HOW TO TRAIN YOUR DEMON

A DEMON-HUNTING
SOCCER MOM
ADVENTURE

USA TODAY BESTSELLING AUTHOR
JULIE KENNER

HOW TO TRAIN YOUR DEMON

A DEMON-HUNTING SOCCER MOM ADVENTURE

USA TODAY BESTSELLING AUTHOR

JULIE KENNER

"Did you notice how the demons were with her?"

For a moment, they were all silent. Then Eric nodded. "I did. I hoped I was wrong."

"You weren't," I told him.

"What?" Laura asked.

"The demons weren't attacking her," I said.

"Don't be ridiculous. Of course they—*oh.*"

"Damn," Cutter said. "You're right."

"And Allie? Did our girl realize she was getting the royal treatment?" Eddie's scowl was severe. I couldn't blame him.

"That's the million dollar question," Eric said.

I shook my head. "No, the million dollar question is why. Why on earth would they leave her alone?"

I met Eric's eyes, terrified of what this meant. "It's not that they're scared of her."

"No," Eric agreed. "It's not."

I closed my eyes and drew a breath. "It's because of what she is. Of what she can do."

DEMON-HUNTING SOCCER MOM

Carpe Demon
California Demon
Demons Are Forever
Deja Demon
The Demon You Know (bonus short story)
Demon Ex Machina
Pax Demonica
Day of the Demon
How To Train Your Demon

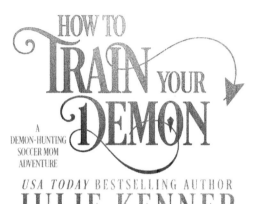

HOW TO TRAIN YOUR DEMON

A
DEMON-HUNTING
SOCCER MOM
ADVENTURE

USA TODAY BESTSELLING AUTHOR

JULIE KENNER

M&O

How to Train Your Demon Copyright © 2022 Julie Kenner

ISBN: 978-1-953572-26-4

Cover Design by T.M. Franklin (images from @FairytaleDesign and @KickAssRenderStock)

Published by Martini & Olive Books

V-2022-3-15P2

Grief is a tricky thing.

For over three long months, my husband has been lying motionless in a hospital bed, fed by nothing more than an intravenous tube, his body hooked up to all sorts of monitors, his mind lost to me.

His bruises have faded. His wounds have healed. And yet he's still gone, trapped inside himself, and all I want to do is give in to the anguish and the fear. To drop to my knees and lose myself in tears and prayers as I try to wrap my fingers around the thin strands of hope that have begun to dissipate like so much mist.

That's what I want to do, but I don't. I can't.

I'm a mom with two kids who need me. More than that, I know what the hospital staff doesn't—that Stuart's comatose state isn't because of a problem in his brain or any physical trauma. His injuries are the mystical kind that happen when you throw yourself into the middle of a demonic ritual, determined to save your wife and daughter—not to mention the world—even if it means sacrificing yourself.

And it worked.

He kept the High Demon Lilith at bay, sending her back to lick her wounds in some Hell dimension. More important, he destroyed her plan to enter Allie.

He saved us.

And, considering the power Lilith could have wielded were she unbound and corporeal, it's fair to say he saved the world.

But at what price?

That's the question that haunted me as I sat on the edge of Stuart's hospital bed, my heart so tight in my chest that I could barely breathe.

With a shaky exhale, I wiped away the tears that had begun to leak down my cheeks, wishing that the same doctors who could so easily pull off emergency heart surgery or cut out cancer had the power to fix him. So far, though, all we had heard was *We just have to wait and see* over and over until all I wanted was to cry or pummel something.

No. The word came firm into my head, and I told myself to listen to it. We *would* figure this out. We had to.

"I love you, Stuart," I said as I wrapped my hand around his limp fingers. "We're going to get you back. We just have to figure out how. It might take a little time, but I promise we will, because we need you. I need you."

I gave his fingers a little squeeze. "But you don't have to wait for us. You can wake up any time. Please, Stuart," I begged. "Please wake up. I don't think I can do this without you. What if I mess everything up? I'm scared. Please, please come back to me."

If this were a movie, he'd squeeze back as the music swelled. Then he'd open his eyes and his lips would curve up right before he said something deep and meaningful, but with an edge of sardonic humor.

This, however, isn't a movie. It's my life. And it's one hell of a complicated one.

My name is Kate Connor, and I'm a newly promoted Level Six Demon Hunter for *Forza Scura*, a secret arm of the Vatican tasked with fighting demons and other evil beasties that prey on our world.

Demons, however, aren't what I'm scared of. Quite the opposite, actually.

"Stuart," I whispered. "Please. What if I can't handle it? What if I crash and burn and get them all killed? I'm a woman who can barely make cereal. How am I supposed to teach a bunch of kids?"

But he remained stubbornly silent, apparently as clueless about the answer as I was.

I needed to figure it out soon, though, because they were heading my way. Five teens coming to San Diablo to join the first class at the soon-to-open *Forza* West Academy, with yours truly as the headmistress. It's not an elite academic academy—trust me when I say that no one would want me heading up a school where calculus and philosophy are tops of the syllabus. Instead, it's a school for training nascent Demon Hunters, including my daughter Allie. Which, frankly, brings up an entirely different level of angst.

"Okay," I said, adding some cheer to my voice. "I get why you're staying quiet, and you're right. I need to believe in myself and my training. I need to remember that it's not just me at the school. We have a great staff, and everyone is doing their part. I'm fine. You're going to be fine. Allie's—"

I stopped, pain shooting up my arm from where he'd squeezed my hand so hard it felt like my bones might shatter.

"Stuart?"

As he lightened his grip, his eyes opened, then rolled back until they were mostly white. "Allie." His voice sounded cracked and broken, but it was strong, and my entire body went cold with the next words he said: "Be careful ... Allie ... isn't...."

"Mom?"

My heart twisted, and I turned around to see Allie, my sixteen-year-old daughter, standing in the doorway, her forehead creased in a frown as she brushed a strand of recently-dyed pink hair away from her eyes. "Mom, what did he mean?"

As I took a step toward her, Eric hurried into the room, then knocked off the rubber tip of his cane, revealing the deadly steel point. "What happened?"

Allie rushed into his arms, and my heart twisted as I

looked at the two standing together, father and daughter looking so much alike.

I'd lost Eric years ago, and it had almost broken me. For these last few months, I'd been living with the fear that I was going to lose my second husband, too.

Now, though...

Well, now I had hope.

"He spoke." My voice sounded strange to my ears. Lost. Amazed. "He squeezed my hand, and he spoke."

Eric's good left eye went wide, the right hidden under a patch. "I'm going to get a doctor." He turned and hurried out of the room as Allie blinked at me. "He said be careful. He said I wasn't—"

I watched as she gathered her emotions. "Mom, am I supposed to be careful? Or are people supposed to be careful of...."

She let the sentence trail off, but it didn't matter. I knew what she meant. I moved to her side and took her hands in mine. "Sweetie, he's in a coma. He shouldn't be talking at all. Who knows what he's thinking or saying? It doesn't mean anything."

That was a lie. Of course, it meant everything.

"Does this mean he's waking up? He was gone, but he said something. He must have seen something. He knows something," she repeated, her voice rising with fear. "Mom. *Mommy.* Stuart knows something about me. That must be it, and what if it's that I'm—"

"Sweetie, no." I tilted her chin so that she was forced to look me in the eyes. "What happened to your dad ... what you're going through ... I know it's all hard. But you are not evil. It is not inside you. We've been over this, baby. That isn't the way it worked."

Her mouth twisted and she pulled roughly away from me. "We don't know that for sure. We can't."

"I do," I said. "I know exactly what you are, and that's wonderful and strong and good."

I meant the words with all my heart, but in truth, she was right. We didn't know anything about her. Not really. We thought we did. We were pretty damn sure, in fact, and even the Vatican agreed that Allie was just Allie, albeit with some handy-dandy superpowers.

But we couldn't be positive. After all, no one could be sure of what was buried inside any person walking this planet. What they wanted, what they were capable of. I've fought hundreds of demons, sure. But that's hardly the extent of the evil in the world. As much as I wished otherwise, most serial killers and terrorists and other bad guys are just human, and there was no way to know if they had that darkness simply by looking. The same with folks living their normal life. We couldn't know if the good inside outweighed the bad. Not until they were tested. Sometimes, not even then.

And that's just a regular person. Allie was different. Made different. And the not knowing has been driving me crazy. How could I live not knowing what my baby was? What she needed? What she might become?

But that was a problem for any mom, not just a mom with a daughter who'd been the product of a secret program to breed a super-strong Demon Hunter. In my heart, I knew there wasn't anything evil about her. But I also knew myself well enough to know that my heart wasn't always right.

Thankfully, I was pulled out of my spinning thoughts when Eric hurried back through the door with the doctor.

"I understand that Stuart spoke?" The physician looked at me, his eyes reflecting that he thought I was nuts.

"He did. Yes. He really did."

I heard his dubious *hmm*, but couldn't see his face, as he was already at Stuart's side, checking his vitals. I watched as he poked and prodded my husband before checking the readout of the various machines attached to Stuart's head and body.

"He squeezed my hand," I said, wanting to make sure this doctor knew everything. "And he said to be careful."

When the doctor turned from the machine to face me again, the disbelief was clear in his eyes. He thought I was nuts.

"What?" I pressed. "What does the machine say? Is he awake now?"

"Nothing has changed." His tone was gentle. As if he was dealing with a crazy person.

"But he spoke. *Something* has changed."

"I heard it, too," Allie said. "He talked. Maybe he woke up for a little bit?"

"It's very rare to temporarily awake from a coma," the doctor explained, as if talking to kindergartners. "Just as the odds of ever waking grow smaller as more time passes. Stuart is already—"

"We know," I snapped, not wanting to hear again that my husband would probably never wake up. "Except he spoke. I heard him. Allie heard him."

The doctor shook his head slowly. "I am truly sorry. I can't explain what happened in here, and I see no sign on any of the readouts that anything *did* happen."

"But—" Allie began.

"*But*," the doctor continued, "you should know that hope can affect what you think you see and hear."

"We did *not*—" Allie began again, taking a step forward. I squeezed her hand, stopping her.

"I understand," I said. "Thank you, Doctor. Maybe … I don't know. Wishful thinking, maybe. And then Allie heard me, and…."

I drifted off, knowing exactly what I heard, but also knowing that there was no way I would convince this doctor.

"Mom, no. He needs to understand. Stuart spoke." She looked at me, her eyes dark with fear and hope. But I shook my head.

"Thank you," I said, just wanting this doctor to go.

"I know you want good news, Mrs. Connor. But it's been almost four months. Your insurance will quit paying soon. I think we need to revisit the idea of a palliative care facility."

Allie tugged free of my hand, then hurried to Eric, who closed his arms around her. I blinked rapidly, fighting the tears that were pricking my eyes. It took a moment for me to answer, and I had to swallow twice before I could force the words out. "Yes, yes, we'll ... we'll let you know by the weekend."

The doctor held my eyes for a moment, then nodded. He didn't have the best bedside manner, and it pissed me off that he didn't believe what I said about Stuart. But I did know that he was a good doctor. And I also understood why he was dubious.

"Again, I'm truly sorry," he said. "I know how difficult this is."

I kept my eyes on Stuart as the doctor left the room, but I turned once I heard the snick of the door clicking shut. Eric was leaning against it, his eye closed, his arm around Allie. After a moment he opened his eye and looked at me. I saw the pain there, and I wanted to run to him.

But I couldn't. I needed to stand beside my husband. I needed to give him everything. And I couldn't even afford to take comfort from the man who used to be my husband, because I was terrified that if I accepted that gift, I'd never be able to push away from him again.

"He's wrong," Allie said. "I know what I heard. And you know what you heard. I know you do."

I nodded. "Of course I do."

Allie's eyes went wide. "Then why did you just let the doctor—"

"Because it's not a coma thing," I told her. "It's a demon thing. And I don't have a clue what to do now."

9

2

"Maybe the doctor's a demon?"

BANG!

"But this is good, right? Waking up? Does that cryptic comment even count as waking up?"

CRASH!

"What does *be careful* mean?"

"Momma?"

"Is it about Lilith? Isn't she gone? She's gone, right?"

"MOMMY!"

"They're really pushing hospice? Does that mean they don't think Stuart will ever—"

"Daddy! When Daddy coming home?"

At the sound of Stuart's name, Timmy stopped yelling and smashing his Duplo blocks all over the living room. Instead, he came running to me, tears forming in those big brown eyes. "Daddy?"

"Daddy's still sick, kiddo," I said as I scooped him up and settled him on my lap. I hugged him close as I bent

10

down to smell his freshly shampooed hair and soak up the sweet relief as everyone stopped shouting questions at me.

And I do mean everyone. They were all sitting right there. *Everyone.*

Or, at least, everyone who counted in my demon-hunting world. Because unless they were hiding in the kitchen, there was no one from the PTA or the mom group from Timmy's day care, or the growing group of women enrolled in the self-defense class I taught at Cutter's studio. And thank goodness for that. My living room really couldn't hold any more people.

"I want Daddy." Timmy squirmed in my lap, his voice small and his little arms tight around my neck. At three, he didn't understand what was going on. All he knew was that his father hadn't been home for a very long time.

"I know, baby," I said. "I want him home, too."

I blinked back tears as I looked over his head at my best friend, Laura, who was sitting on the sofa next to her daughter Mindy, with Allie right there with them. Laura had been my cohort in all things domestic back before my demon-hunting past turned into my demon-hunting present. Thankfully, our daughters became besties, and while Mindy and Allie bonded over boys and weird video games and more boys, Laura and I had bonded over carpools, PTA, domestic drama, and large glasses of white wine after the kids fell asleep.

That was then. These days we bonded over deciphering demonic texts and trying to figure out new and efficient ways to tell if the new guy behind the dry-cleaning counter really was a demon or if he just had exceptionally poor oral hygiene.

Honestly, it's nice that our relationship keeps evolving. And that our girls are still besties, even after all they've been through.

I'd called Laura from the car on the way home from the hospital to ask her to gather everyone at my house. I'd made the mistake of telling her a few of the high points, which she'd obviously passed onto the group.

Thus the barrage of questions before I'd barely even had a chance to gather my thoughts.

I took a moment to glance around the room at the rest of my ragtag team. Eddie, the curmudgeonly octogenarian ex-demon-hunter who'd become a mentor to me and a grandfather to my kids. Eliza, the nineteen-year-old cousin I never knew existed until she tracked me down in Rome on my vacation this past summer. Cutter, the ex-military martial arts instructor with action-hero good looks who's now dating Laura. And Jared, the dark-haired seventeen-year-old vampire—give or take a hundred years—who both fell for my daughter and betrayed her.

I'd forgiven him, though. He was protecting his sister, after all. And, in the end, he's the reason Stuart's still alive.

Finally, there's Eric. Allie's father. My first love. My demon-hunting partner at *Forza*. And my friend. Honestly, when kids say their relationships are complicated, they really have no idea...

"Kate?" Laura's gentle voice prods me from my thoughts. "What did the doctor say? Does he think it's a sign that Stuart's going to wake up?"

"We should start from the top," Eric said, stepping into the role of co-chair for this meeting. Un-retired from demon hunting like me, that made him my unofficial second in command.

Not that he'd ever meant to retire. More like involuntarily pulled out when he'd been killed back when Allie was nine. Back when he was my husband, Eric Crowe, and before he returned to life in the body of another man five years later.

Now the world knew him as former high school chemistry teacher David Long. Allie finally knew him again as Daddy (though never in public), Timmy called him Uncle David (and maybe one day we'd explain that he was really Eric) and despite a recent and shaky detente, Stuart didn't call him much at all.

Honestly, their lack of communication was fine by me. Or it had been. Right then, I'd happily have them yelling at each other, if only because that would mean that Stuart was alive and well.

I heard a little sobbing noise and realized it came from me. "Sorry."

"Katie," Eric said gently. "It's okay. Take your time. Or I can tell the story if you'd rather."

I shook my head. "I'm good. I've got this." I looked around at the faces in the room. With the exception of Laura, Mindy, and Eliza, everyone in the room had been present at the ceremony where the High Demon Lilith had tried to enter Allie. It had been a hellish battle, but in the end, Stuart had saved her.

But that victory hadn't been without a price.

"You all know he's been in a coma since that fight at the stone table," I began, then reminded them of the rest. How he'd sacrificed himself to save Allie, knowing full well that if it worked, he would either die or go insane. He only survived because Jared had pulled him free at the last minute.

Survived, yes. But he wasn't truly alive. Instead, he was trapped in his body, and for all I knew he really had gone insane. Maybe he was suffering a horrible Love-craftian kind of madness that tormented him day in and day out.

I couldn't let myself believe that, though. Jared had bought him time. And Stuart would come back, well and whole. At least I hoped so.

Once again, I wiped away a tear, then drew a breath and continued. "We visit him every day and talk to him. Today, he squeezed my—"

"Hold up there, girlie. You skipped a bit."

I glanced toward Eddie and shook my head. "No, I—"

"What were you talking about when he squeezed?"

Even in his eighties, Eddie was as sharp as they came. Except when he wanted to be intentionally obtuse. Right then, though, he was right. "The school," I admitted. "I was talking about being nervous. Because I am," I added defensively, looking at everyone in turn and silently daring them to judge me for being freaked out by the prospect of taking responsibility for the training of young *Forza* Demon Hunters. And, yes, I knew perfectly well that it wasn't all on me.

Except that it really felt like it was all on me.

"That's it?" Eddie pressed. "Just boo-hoo, I'm a nervous Nelly and he squeezed your hand?"

"No," I snapped. "I was rallying. I said that—"

"She said that she'd be fine," Allie interrupted. "And that the students would be fine. And that I'd—" Her voice broke, and she looked down at her shoes, her voice dropping to such a whisper that I had to strain to hear. "That's when he did it. He squeezed her hand, and he said my name. And he said *be careful.* He said *Allie isn't.*"

"Isn't what?" Mindy asked at the same time Eliza posed that exact question.

"Safe," Allie snapped, the fear in her voice breaking my heart. "Good. Right."

"He said all that?" Eliza asked.

"No, but that's what he must have meant. That somehow it worked and Lilith got inside me, just like she'd been trying to do all along. And she's hiding now, and I'm not really me. Or I never was—not after what happened when Daddy was little. And then with me in Rome. I'm dangerous because they made me that way."

The words poured out of her, breaking my heart. "Maybe that's not what they were trying to do, but they did, and now Stuart knows, and he's trying to warn—"

"Allie, baby—"

"*No.* He said be careful, and he was talking about me, and—"

"*Stop it.*" With preternatural speed, Jared crossed the room to where Allie sat beside Mindy. "Just take a breath, okay? You're confused and you're scared, and who could blame you? But you are *not* evil. So, yeah, you got a shit deal with Father Donnelly's wacko plan to create some super-strong Demon Hunter—you and your dad," he added, glancing over at Eric. "But it *worked*. You're special Allie. Not bad. At least not unless *you* are bad. You've got serious strength and power and who knows what else. So use it, right? Use it for good. *Be* good. Because there's nothing evil inside you. Trust me. I know evil."

I watched him, this ancient boy, as he knelt in front of my daughter and took her hands. "Do you think I would have helped save you if you were bad? Do you think I would have sacrificed my chance to find Celia?" His voice broke, and I knew he was thinking about the fact that after the battle he no longer had the occasional telepathic contact with his little sister, who was imprisoned at some unknown location.

He shook it off, straightening his shoulders as he continued. "You've got this, Allie. You do. And Stuart loves you. He knows what you're going to be up against. He wants *you* to be careful. And so do I."

"He's right," Mindy said, putting her arm around her bestie. "Even when you're being a bitch, you're not actually evil."

"Mindy!" Laura chided, but it worked, and Allie smiled and shoulder-bumped her friend.

"Thanks. I guess I believe you guys. Or I'm trying to.

I mean, I did feel her leave that night once it was all over. Or, I thought I did. But sometimes I just…"

"Freak out," Jared said. "Yeah. Who wouldn't? You're one of a kind, Alison Crowe. And you've got this."

He waited for her small smile, then returned to where he'd been sitting by Cutter, who in his typical style, was silently absorbing everything. Now, the former SEAL turned to me. "But the doctor doesn't think this is a sign he's waking up?"

I shook my head. "He said there was nothing on monitors to indicate that."

"So how did he speak?"

"Mom said it was a demon thing," Allie told Cutter. "Not a coma thing." Her brow furrowed as her attention returned to me. "What does that mean, anyway?"

"Oh! Oh, I know!" Mindy bounced in her seat, her hand thrust high as if trying to grab the teacher's attention. I had a strange premonition of what it was going to be like once we got the school open and actually had classes.

"You don't have to be called on," I told her. "Just tell us."

"You're thinking that being saved from death in the middle of some dark mystical ceremony gave him some sort of awareness. I read about that in one of the books that Father Corletti sent from the *Forza* library at the Vatican. There's not a lot of case studies—and they're all like super-old—but there was this saint, and he—" She broke off, waving her words away.

"Anyway, that's what happened, right? Stuart touched the stone table when it was imbued with Lilith's power, but then his blood stopped the ritual so that she couldn't jump into Allie. And Jared pulled him out before it killed him."

"That's right," I tell her as Timmy slid off my lap and headed toward the kitchen. I consider following, but this was Important Stuff. I could clean up kitchen destruction later.

"Question," Cutter said. "Is there a chance Lilith is in Stuart?"

I glanced toward Eric, disturbed by the question. I'd told myself it wasn't possible, but now that Cutter had raised it...

"No," Eric said firmly. "Lilith's a High Demon. Her power is too great to allow her to become corporeal within a living human host without a lot of other stuff happening first. Besides, over the last few months we've practically drowned Stuart in holy water."

"A lot of stuff *did* happen," Cutter said, then held up his hands. "Not saying that means Lilith's in Stuart. Just trying to get clarity."

"I understand that," Eric said. "But again, holy water. Plus, the ceremony allowed the stone table to be a conduit for Lilith to get into Allie. Lilith could enter Allie—and a High Demon could enter me—because of ... well, because of what Father Donnelly and my parents did when I was a child. But that makes Allie and me unique."

"I thought demons could enter any dead person

whose soul didn't fight to keep them out," Laura said. "That's how you've always explained it. That demons want to live in this world. To enjoy the pleasures of being mortal. And when someone dies, there's a short opportunity for them to slip in. The person's soul can fight to keep them out, but only the faithful usually win that fight."

"Gold star," I said. "That's exactly right."

"But those folks are dead," Mindy said. "Stuart's alive."

"We've seen High Demons in humans," Allie reminded me. "Goramesh, remember? I mean, I didn't know it at the time, but you told me, and—"

"That's because Judge Larson consented. He allowed the demon to basically time-share. We're talking about *pushing* into a body. That's a lot harder for regular demons. And impossible—or at least pretty much impossible—for High Demons because they're hard to contain in the flesh."

"But Eric and Allie could host one," Eliza added, "because Eric's parents basically shoved a demon inside of him, and since he's Allie's father, that made her different, too."

"That's the theory," I said. The truth was, I didn't want to think about this. As much as we knew, even *Forza* didn't know everything. Maybe there was a way Lilith could be in Stuart despite the holy water not burning him.

"Could be just a piece of her," Eddie said, his caterpillar eyes drawing together as he seemingly read my mind. "That boy might have a piece of that bitch demon shoved inside him somewhere."

"But the holy water," Laura said as I shook my head vigorously.

"No. No, I don't believe it." I felt tears start to fill my eyes. I *didn't* believe it. I'd never even heard of that. Demons didn't break up into pieces. Did they?

I wanted to ask Eddie—maybe High Demons could —but right then I couldn't stand the thought of anything but hope in my head.

I was just about to tell Eddie that when Timmy came to me and held out a Chips Ahoy bag. "Momma want a cookie?"

I laughed, the sound more like a sob, then pulled him into my lap. "Yeah. Momma would love a cookie."

I drew him close, hugging him tight as the room fell silent, Eddie's dark suggestion hanging over all of us.

"Here's the thing," Eric finally said. "At the end of the day, we can't really know anything for certain. All we know is what's in the records that have been kept over centuries. Things the Churches and demonologists and Demon Hunters have learned over the years and put down to paper. But the demons never gave us a manual."

"So everything we think we know could be wrong," Jared said, coming over to take the cookie that Timmy was holding out to him.

"Lilith isn't in Stuart," Allie said, lifting her chin. "I told you I felt her go. Daddy did, too, right?" She looked at Eric, and he nodded. "And holy water doesn't bother him. So it's all okay. We just have to wait for him to get better. And he—he warned me to be careful, so I will."

I knew that she was still worried that she was the thing others need to be careful of, and I was proud of her for not raising that again. For understanding we all needed to find some calm.

"So I guess we should start looking for a hospice," Laura said. "I can help. Or you can call Coastal Mists. They're demon-free these days."

"*Harumph.*" That from Eddie. Coastal Mists could have been personally blessed by the Pope himself, and Eddie still wouldn't trust the place. Honestly, I'm not sure I could either.

"I can't put him in one of those places. They're depressing. And dangerous." Any place where people die regularly—nursing homes, hospices, hospitals—are regular stomping grounds for incorporeal demons looking for a home. The last thing I wanted was a pissed-off Lilith to order a newly-corporeal demon to take out my husband for spite. And that, I realized, was a very likely scenario.

"True enough," Eric said when I told the gang my fears.

"Why not here?" Allie asked. "And we hire one of those home health care nurses?"

"Not a bad idea," I agreed. Except for the whole *where will the money for this nurse come from* part of the equation. My salary from *Forza* hasn't exactly put me on the *Fortune 500* list, and Stuart's income dropped considerably when he and his friend Bernie decided to go into the real estate business. He assured me that would change once they had more traction, but meanwhile things had been tight.

I didn't bother telling any of that to Allie, though. She hardly needed to know that lately our contributions to her college fund have been on the scrimpy side. A fact that I justified because we were paying for things like the mortgage and food. And because I wasn't entirely sure my daughter was going to go to college, as much as I wanted her to. She had a path now, albeit a dangerous one.

Mostly I didn't say any of that because her words had given me an idea. *Why not here?* Well, *here* might not be possible, but *there* could work out just fine. "The school," I said to the group. "What if we put Stuart in a room at the academy?"

For a moment, no one said anything. Then Eric nodded. "That's actually brilliant. Plus, *Forza* should cover the bills, just like they're paying for the conversion into a school and all our teaching salaries."

"That's right," Laura said. "Stuart's in a coma from fighting a demon."

"And that day will be revelatory for those of us who'll be teaching," Eric said.

"And those of us who'll be doing both," Jared added. As a vampire, he was a hell of a fighter, and was going to help Cutter with physical training. He'd also teach a class on vampires and other supernatural creatures—fact versus mythology, how to vet a vampire as friend or foe, that kind of thing. Other than that, though, he was going to be a student, too. That had been his idea. "Celia and I never had anyone to teach us," he'd told me. "Maybe if we had, we could have seen Lilith coming. Could have fought better."

Honestly, his reasons didn't matter because I wanted him at the school. He cared for Allie. I knew he would never hurt her—at least not physically. And he'd protect her with his life.

I forced my attention back to Eric's suggestion. "So you're saying *Forza* will pay for Stuart's care?"

"We've already talked with Father Corletti about making sure we have skilled medical staff on site," Cutter said. "We have to ensure the students' well-being. And the staff's."

"And you forget how massive the budget for *Forza Scura* is, even with the recent cuts."

"But *Forza*'s already funding the remodel," I protested. The school is going to be located in the Great-water Mansion, a cool-yet-spooky old mansion once owned by a man who dabbled in the occult. Stuart ran across it when he and Bernie first got into real estate, and it had been so run down, the price was next to nothing.

He'd intended to buy it for our family, despite the fact that it was about a billion times too big for our little group of four. Then when Father Corletti started making noises about me training potential Demon Hunters ... well, there was the mansion, looking remarkably like a potential boarding school.

Fortunately, Father Corletti loved the idea, and for months construction crews had been working overtime.

It must have cost a fortune. Would they really add to that? Could they?

"They can, and they will," Eric said in response to my question. "I'll call Father Corletti myself, but you know I'm right. For one thing, it's the right thing to do. For another, we all know that we need to keep an eye on Stuart. He might say something else, and if he does, we need to hear it."

"So we're moving?" Allie said, looking from me to Timmy and then to Eric.

"That's up to your mom," Eric said, then turned to me. "Had you and Stuart decided?"

I drew in a breath, then nodded even though the truth was that we hadn't decided anything yet. Moving full-time into the school meant leaving the house that I loved with the backyard that connected to Laura and Mindy's backyard. It meant really—like *really*—being the headmistress for this new school. Because if I was living on site, then there was no way to escape that reality, no matter how unprepared I might feel.

And what if I wanted to come back? This house would have a renter, and I'd be trapped. Plus, was I really ready to make this my life? Timmy's life? Because if I moved, then he moved, too. And once that happened, wheels would be set in motion. Wheels that would almost assuredly move my little boy away from other options and firmly toward the family business.

Oh, God.

"Kate," Eric said gently, "Timmy will always have options. And the house will stay like it is. I promise."

"Oh." I wasn't surprised that Eric knew what I was thinking, but I didn't understand what he was saying. "How? For that matter, how do you know?"

"We talked about it. Stuart and me, about the house. I'm renting it. And Eddie's going to stay here with me."

Allie jumped up. "You're not staying at the school? Neither of you?"

He shook his head. "Not at first. Maybe later. Father Corletti thought it made the most sense for me to be off-site."

"Why?"

But Eric only shrugged without answering. Didn't matter. I understood. The school was supposed to be my baby, but if Eric was on site full-time—the man I spent my youth training and working and fighting with—then I'd use him as a crutch, letting him guide my decisions at a time when the school needed one voice.

Plus, it was going to be strange enough for Allie to have her mother be in charge. Having her "uncle" living on site, too, would lead to that annoying kind of finger-pointing. No matter what, Allie was going to stand out. No sense making it worse.

"I get it," I said, and Allie looked between us with a scowl. "It makes sense," I told her. "At least until we're settled. Plus, this gives you a place to come hang out with your dad where you don't have to remember to call him Uncle David."

"Fine," she said, though she sounded less than thrilled. "But you're not moving either?" She turned her attention to Eddie.

"Can't. What? You think you're gonna move that cat into a place that size?"

I glanced around for Kabit, our grumpy, opinionated tomcat, but he was nowhere to be seen. Still, Eddie was right. Kabit was a creature of habit. He'd hate the move.

"Besides, I got Rita to think about," Eddie continued, referring to the woman he was dating. "Live there and it'll be hard to keep the truth from her. Not without lying even more than I do, and that don't seem fair."

"You really haven't told her?" I'd always wondered how much Rita knew. Among other things, she'd seen Eric lose it at Allie's fifteenth birthday party—he'd been having demonic possession issues—and I'd always assumed that Eddie had broken down and given her the full scoop.

"Come on, girlie. You think I'd do that without telling you? Asking you?"

"I—well, maybe?"

"*Hmmph.*"

"It's just that you two have gotten so close."

He pats the arms of his recliner. "Which is why I'm staying here."

"Whatever," Allie said, then crossed her arms and stared down Mindy. "What about you? Are you staying in your house, too?"

Mindy turned to Laura. "I'm not, am I? I want to live at the school."

"I know. But I'm going to stay in the house. Well, *we* are." She smiled at Cutter, who winked as Mindy squealed with delight. "But we'll both be at the school during working hours."

"Except when I'm at the studio," Cutter said. "I'm keeping a few limited classes, including yours," he added nodding to me as he referenced the women's self-defense class I was teaching.

"Well, good," I said, happy for the two of them. And a little envious at their relatively normal love life. "I'm glad you're keeping the house. That means it will be even easier to bring Timmy back to see his friends."

I sighed , letting these new arrangements settle in my bones. It was all happening so fast ... but even so, I couldn't help but think that the whirlwind was moving in the right direction.

"Can Mindy and I stop going to Coronado now?" Allie asked. "We want to get settled at the school before the others kids get here. And Daddy quit a week ago."

"No more Coronado," I agreed, knowing that if I said otherwise, I'd have a battle on my hands. Besides, I really could use both their help.

Technically, the school doesn't open until the winter semester, but Father Corletti suggested we start midway through this semester with a smaller batch of kids. That way, we could get our feet wet without wrangling three dozen students, which is the school's maximum capacity. Although if I have anything to say about it, we'll limit the first full class to eighteen. Considering I'd never wrangled more than two at a time—three if you count Mindy— I'm all about wading in.

Since that had seemed like a good idea, Father

Corletti put the wheels in motion, and we have five students arriving in ten days.

I glanced around at everybody in the room. "So, have we covered everything? I guess we just need to talk to Father Corletti and find out if there's a nurse or someone who can move in early to monitor Stuart."

When the school opens, we'll have medical staff for the kids—as well as a kitchen staff for meals. Housekeeping and maintenance are already on site, thank goodness. And all are *Forza* approved, know what we're doing, and have been trained in the basics of demon identification.

"I'll call," Eric said, but I shook my head.

"No, that's my job. And the nurse is for my husband. I should do it." I moved across the room to where I left my cell phone. As I closed my hand around it, it rang, and I actually jumped. Some kind of Hunter, right?

As I silently cursed myself, I glanced at the screen, then smiled with delight when I saw the caller—Father Corletti.

"Father," I said, answering on speaker. "I'm so glad to hear from you." The Vatican-based head of *Forza Scura* had practically raised me after I was found wandering the streets of Rome when I was only four. He's like a father to me, and I mean that in all the meanings of the word.

"Ah, *mia cara*, I am so sorry that I must take away some of that joy. There has been an attack. Two of your new students are dead."

28

3

I didn't realize that Eric had moved to my side until I felt his arms around me, holding me steady despite my knees that had gone weak.

I met his eyes, his face looking as sad and broken as I felt.

I took a moment to make sure my voice was steady, then said, "Tell us exactly what happened."

"As you know, we had identified over thirty possible students from all over the globe. For this initial half-semester, we selected five from the United States to make travel and acclimation easier.

"A few days ago, they convened in Nashville with *Forza* representatives for a more complete briefing about the school than they may have received when originally scouted. Each was offered a chance to decline, of course."

"After getting more of an idea of what was in store for them," I said. This process was all new to me. As an orphan, I'd been thrust into *Forza* at the age of four, training with other lost children. I didn't realize until very late that *Forza* had an actual recruitment process whereby it actively sought out talent.

"Marcus ran that meeting, right? Is he okay?"

The son of one of my trainers at *Forza*, Marcus Giatti grew up to be a talented fighter—and trainer —himself.

"Indeed, and he is well. As you know, the potential students had already been heavily recruited in their home states. But once they met each other we wanted to ensure the group melded, and that each student understood what the school would teach and how it would be run. Marcus flew from Italy to conduct that meeting and then to bring the students to you."

"And somebody didn't like it?" Seemed like an overreaction, but you never knew how someone would react when they finally understood what it meant to live in a world full of demons.

"No. That was not where the tragedy occurred. From Nashville, they began the journey to California. That was three days ago."

"With Marcus?"

"No. There was an emergency—a demon infestation that he had to handle. The local archbishop assigned a deacon to escort them. This man did not know about *Forza*, and the students were instructed not to speak of it. As far as the deacon knew, the five were heading for an academic camp. They got as far as Tulsa, and then they were attacked."

"A demon?" I squeezed Eric's hand.

"Yes." He sounded tired. Older than I'd ever heard him sound. "But she was also one of the students."

"Oh, dear God."

"The demon infested a fourteen-year-old girl. Jessica. I never met the child, but Father Donnelly found her when he was in New York. Obviously she was not a demon then. We don't know how death came upon her, but clearly the opportunity for invasion by the beast occurred."

"And no one noticed any unusual behavior during the trip?" Eric asked.

"I presume that she was doing her very best to fit in. Or she was not turned until Nashville when she took out the deacon and seriously injured another student, Dani, a girl from South Carolina."

I put the phone down, still on speaker, and hugged myself, looking around the room at the shocked faces of my friends and family. "Go on."

"The demon was stopped. Another student—a sixteen-year-old boy by the name of Bruce jumped into the fray. He was too late to save the deacon, and Dani died while they were waiting for an ambulance. Still, Bruce managed to overpower the demon. He used a pen to stab her in the eye and release the demon."

"Thank God," I said. "If that demon had gotten the rest of them..."

"Yes," Father Corletti said. "We promised them sanctuary. An education and training. But the first thing they witness is death."

"They will have to learn about it sooner or later,"

Eric said. "But I'm so terribly sorry that it had to be sooner."

"Bruce sounds like he's going to be our star student," Cutter said. "But their parents. Have they been notified? They must be devastated."

"It is both a blessing and a tragedy that these children who are coming to you have no families."

"What do you mean?" Allie asked.

"He means they're like me," I said. "Orphans. Kids in the system. That's the way *Forza* usually works." The fact is almost all Demon Hunters come to *Forza* as children of retired Hunters, novitiates or seminarians who realized their true calling was to fight, or rejects from society.

The latter group was the largest by far. With no parents and no family, it made it easier to do what had to be done. And those Hunters had no family that a demon could attack as a pressure point.

I learned that one the hard way, but I also knew that my family gave me strength. More than that, I knew that *Forza* truly had been my family back in the day when I lived in the dorms in Rome.

"I have family," Allie said firmly, looking at everyone in the room, but stopping at Eliza, who nodded. "And we'll make them feel part of our family."

"Damn right," Eliza said, as Eric caught my eye and smiled.

But that brief moment of solidarity evaporated soon enough, and Eric's face turned harsh. "We should have collected them after Marcus got called away. Not just sent them with a deacon who knew nothing about fighting demons. They should have had a Hunter as a chaperone."

"I don't disagree with you," Father Corletti said, "but hindsight is more clear. As far as we knew, there was no need for protection. It's not as if we are advertising the school."

He was right about that. We didn't have ads in the back of magazines. We weren't putting flyers up at local churches. But at the same time, we were spreading the word. Every time a priest aware of *Forza* talked to a kid in the system, the word got out.

And, true, there weren't that many priests who actually knew about *Forza*, but it only took one. "Do you think the potential students who say no are going to keep it a secret? Do you think that the ones who were recruited really understand the importance of silence? One wrong word to a friend, even an entirely innocent word and...."

I trailed off, feeling a little sick. "We messed this up, Father. We really did."

"You are right, *mia cara*. But all we can do is move forward, pray for our charges, and learn from our mistakes."

"That's not all," Eric said. "I can bring them in. I can protect them. You said they're in Tulsa? I can get on the next plane there."

"There is no need. Marcus will be landing there within the hour."

"You mentioned him before. Who's Marcus?" The

question came from Mindy who'd been sitting next to Allie and listening intently to the conversation.

"Marcus Giatti. He's one of the trainers who's coming to work at the school," I told her. "He's been working for *Forza* at the Vatican for the last few years."

"Oh!" She turned to Allie. "Isn't he the one you said was—" She cut herself off with a sideways glance at Jared.

Allie rolled her eyes. "Yeah. I said he was cute. He is."

I started to comment that Marcus, in his late twenties, was too old for either of them. Then I remembered that Allie and Jared had started to date—something I was still uncomfortable with, but mostly because my daughter was dating, not because he was a vampire. Still, though he looked seventeen, he was actually more than a hundred years older than her, so maybe it was best to just stay silent on the whole age and dating thing.

"Marcus will be meeting the surviving students at the cathedral in Tulsa," Father Corletti continued. "They will stay the night in the church's guest house, then fly into Los Angeles in the morning before traveling up to San Diablo. They should arrive at the school mid-afternoon."

"Why not just fly straight here? We could go pick them up at the airport."

"Father Donnelly is in Los Angeles. He will debrief the students, then accompany them to San Diablo."

Once again, Eric and I locked eyes. He looked as unhappy as I felt.

Father Donnelly was not on my favorite person list, nor Eric's, and Father Corletti knew it. Donnelly has had

his fingers in *Forza* for decades and he was in deep with
the plot to breed a next gen Demon Hunter. He's
responsible for what happened to both Eric and Allie,
and as far as I was concerned, his experiments were
horrific. He was playing with forces he didn't understand. Playing with children and bloodlines. Playing with
their lives without any understanding of the conse-
quences.

I looked at my daughter. My beautiful daughter.
What Father Donnelly had done to Eric had trickled
down to her. And, yes, his horrific program may have
culminated in the extraordinary powers that recently
manifested in her, but that's a good result that happened
despite his bad acts. And because of what he did, she'd
lost so much, including years that she could have spent
with her father. More than that, she no longer knew who
she was, and had no understanding of what was inside
of her.

And all of that meant that I wanted Father Donnelly
far away from Allie.

I remembered a piece of paper I'd seen in Eliza's
things when she moved up from San Diego. Some
genealogical papers that her mom—my aunt—had kept.
And right there on one branch, as clear as day, was the
name Donnelly.

I didn't know why. I didn't know if he was really part
of our family. And I didn't know how he might be
related to Eliza or to me. But the idea that I might share
blood with that man was not something I wanted to
think about.

But if he was here, at *Forza* West, I knew that I'd be hard pressed to think about anything else.

"I don't want him working at this school," I said. "Eric can go get the kids. He doesn't need to come. And he certainly doesn't need to stay."

"He does need to come," Father Corletti said. "But he won't be at the school. He'll be at St. Mary's. Father Donnelly is the new priest for the San Diablo parish."

4

"I'm going to get you," I shouted, racing to catch up with the little demon who was barreling across the school's massive entrance hall. "I'm totally going to get you!"

"No, Momma!" Timmy giggled as he pedaled his tricycle madly and continued across the room, making a sharp left turn into the hallway towards the kitchen area.

I stopped, breathing deep. I work out—obviously, with the whole demon-hunting thing—but I've been working since the crack of dawn to prepare for the students' arrival this afternoon and get Stuart settled in his room.

Father Corletti had agreed that *Forza* should cover the cost of Stuart's care, and the hospital was able to arrange for the transfer today. I was glad, of course, but everything was happening at a breakneck pace. We still didn't have a nurse for Stuart, but his various machines were hooked up to the school's alarm system, so we'd know if anything changed. Plus, Eddie's girlfriend, Rita, had agreed to sit with him this first day. Considering it was becoming clear that she'd be spending a lot of time here, I had to wonder how long it would take before Eddie broke down and told her the truth about the school—and the students we were teaching.

Bottom line, I was exhausted. But I hadn't spent enough time with my three year old, and demons notwithstanding, he deserved a little mommy time. Thus the wild chase through the halls of the Greatwater mansion.

And there are a lot of halls.

It's absolutely humongous, and is nestled at the top of a hill with an exceptional view of pretty much everything in San Diablo from eastern hills to the western beach. The grounds are gorgeous, and include a cemetery, which seems apropos for demon hunting.

Inside, visitors arrive in to a cavernous entrance hall will windows that let in plenty of light. As for schoolrooms, there are more than enough for teaching and living. The upstairs ballroom—one of several—is now the main training room, with a convenient outdoor staircase to the yard for outdoor workouts and another indoor staircase that leads to the mansion's tunnel system that provides access all the way across the property to where the main kitchen is located.

The library, located downstairs, is still the library, with floor to ceiling bookshelves and several freestanding shelves already filled with many occult-related titles left by the most infamous previous resident. Eric was in heaven when he saw it. He's already moved in his own massive private collection, and his ongoing project is cataloging the additional books. I was pretty sure he thought he'd died and gone to heaven.

Multiple wings feature massive bedrooms, each with an attached smaller room that had presumably been used as a sitting area or nursery. Those are for the teaching staff who live on site.

As for the students, they were located in the former servants' living area, several wings lined with rooms. They'd come furnished with musty twin beds and moldering dressers, all of which we were replacing in order to provide the kids with the best dorm experience. And—bonus for them—they're near the kitchen and the dining area, a fact that proved out when Timmy zipped his trike in there. He was well ahead of me, but I was certain he was riding circles around the very expensive commercial ovens and stovetops.

"Out of the kitchen, mister. You know the rules." I heard the *squeak squeak* of the wheels on his trike as he turned his vehicle around, then the faster squeak as he pedaled madly. A moment later, I saw him cross the huge dining room — which we had furnished with three long dining table — and emerged back into the entry hall to join me, grinning like a fiend.

"He really is a demon," Laura said from behind me. I turned to face her and she cocked her head. "He reminds me of those two creepy girls in *The Shining*. And honestly, this house reminds me of that hotel."

As if to punctuate her comment, she looked down at

the huge tiles inlaid with all sorts of strange symbols that, hopefully, aren't part of a ritual to summon demons.

"Thank you," I said. "Thanks so much. That's just what I need to hear before I move my family into this place."

She shrugged. "At least you're a family of Demon Hunters." She grinned at me, and I rolled my eyes. "Hey, I'm just saying. I mean with this place's history, anything's possible."

To be honest, I can't say that she's wrong. The house had a somewhat checkered past, what with once being occupied by Theophilus Monroe, a dabbler in the occult, who was apparently inclined to bring the house into his obsession as well. "It's been checked out," I assured her. "Totally *Forza* approved."

"Glad to hear it. I have enough demons in my life. Don't need them in my workday, too."

"Except now your workday actually is about demons."

She frowned, considering. "Good point. Guess I should've taken that job at Walmart."

"You're a hoot."

"I really am, but nice of you to notice."

I rolled my eyes. "Where are the kids?" I'd been so busy with Timmy and fixing up Stuart's room, which primarily consisted of me trying to get his television to work since I thought the sound of voices would help bring him back to himself, that I'd lost track of Allie and Eliza and Mindy. "They're not bothering the assembly people, are they?"

"I doubt it," Laura said. "Those guys are in the dorms putting together the desks. I can't imagine they want to hang out in their dorms with the workmen."

"Good point."

The dorms had been repainted, carpeted, and almost completely furnished over a month ago. But the company we bought the furniture from had forgotten the student desks. Now they're here, with a team of nine doing the assembly work.

"So where are they?" I pressed.

"Allie and Eliza are supposed to be training with Jared in the studio. And Mindy's in the tech center on the computer."

"There's a whole tech team from the Vatican coming to make sure we have access to all the *Forza* databases on a secure line," I reminded her. "What's she doing now?"

"Something for Jared. I think they're trying to figure out where Celia could be based on the various visions he had."

"Good luck with that. From the way he described it, he didn't see many landmarks."

"I know. But she said she wants to try."

"Poor guy." I meant what I said, but I was also worried about what might happen if we did find Celia.

Jared's a good guy, despite the whole being a vampire thing, but I wasn't certain about his sister. For one thing, she was only ten when she was turned. And while I knew that a vampire's mind continued to develop even when its body didn't, in my experience the vamps turned when they were young children never developed the kind of judgment that older vampires have. At seventeen, Jared would have been considered a man in the last century. But Celia—well, she would have still been a coddled child.

Add that to the years of torture that Lilith put her through, and I was worried.

Even more, I was concerned that—if she even was alive—that Lilith's minions were feeding her human blood. Vampires can survive just fine on animal blood, but they crave human blood. And, like an addict, when they drink it, they crave more. Some can fight the urges until they pass. But to others, the longing becomes so intense they lose themselves to nothing but the blood and the kill.

I feared that Celia would fall into the latter group, and I was afraid that even Jared would be unable to wean her off to the point where the students would be safe around her.

Still, I supposed it was too early to worry. We didn't even know if the poor girl was still alive, much less where to find her. Which pushed Celia way down on my very long list of Things To Do and Worry About.

"She's got to have issues," Laura said, apparently having followed my thoughts.

"I know. It worries me. But if we do find her, I don't think we could refuse to bring her in. I mean, she's Jared's sister, no matter how much it would make me nervous."

"I get it," Laura said. "Jared's a hero."

"He sure is." I shoved my hand into my pockets. "I think Allie's really falling for him."

Laura's brows rose. "You think?"

I shrugged. "I've been living in denial," I admitted. "The idea of Allie and a vampire. I thought she'd get over it."

"She still might," Laura said. "There are definite downsides. The age difference, for one thing, though that certainly doesn't seem to bother him. And I'm guessing she forgets about it since he looks so young. And even with his century, he pulls off a teen well."

"He does," I agreed. Camouflage, I supposed, since I knew that he could slide into the persona of an elder statesman, too.

"But if they really end up together, she would age and he wouldn't," Laura said. "That's got to be inconvenient. I don't care how romanticized the movies make it seem."

"Oh, *Highlander*," I said. "We haven't seen that one in forever."

"Not a vampire."

"Still. *Highlander.*"

She laughed. "We should watch it in Stuart's room," Laura suggested. "Doesn't he think it's totally cringy? Maybe that would wake him up."

I laughed. "We can play it really loud. If that won't wake him up, nothing will."

"I can think of a few of Timmy's videos that might do the trick," Laura retorted, then grinned at me.

I reached over and squeezed her hand. "Thanks."

43

"Honestly, I don't know how you do it."

"I don't have any choice. And I've got good friends to support me."

"Yeah," she said. "I get that."

I turned in a circle, suddenly aware of the quiet. "Where's Timmy?"

She twisted around as well, taking in the area. "Oh, hell. I told you he was a demon."

"I'll start here," I said, telling myself not to panic. It's a big house, and he's just exploring. "You take the dorm area? He might be watching the workers. And if we don't find him soon, we should ask the housekeeping staff to help."

"Deal," she said, as I made a mental note to remind myself of all their names and to introduce Timmy to each of them, just in case he slams into one of them with his trike. "Text when you find the rugrat."

"Will do," I agreed, then sprinted off to find my missing son.

5

I told myself that I was absolutely one-hundred percent certain that nothing bad had happened to Timmy. Except I wasn't certain. Not really. And I was starting to get to that point where I feared that I needed pull everyone in the house into service. And then, once we found him, I needed to invest in a little bell for him to wear around his neck.

I told myself that any mother would be frantic if her little boy disappeared into a humongous mansion that still had sections under construction. My fear was completely rational.

Except it wasn't the house that worried me. No, I was worried about the things that go bump in the night. Or, more specifically, the things that go bump in the night *and* the day.

"Timmy!" I called again at the top of my lungs.

He didn't respond, but this time I did get an answer. "Kate? Kate, can you come up here?"

It took me a second to recognize the voice, then I realized it was Rita Walker, Eddie's lady friend.

"Kate?" she called again.

"On my way!" My heart pounded hard in my chest. She'd either found a dead body in the upstairs hallway, or she'd found my son. Hopefully not both.

I cringed. Hunting demons made for a particularly morbid sense of humor, and I didn't like the fact that I was displaying it to myself about my own little boy.

I took the stairs two at a time, seriously less gracefully than the movie stars who I knew had come down that same ornate set of stairs in fabulous ball gowns.

Once I reached the landing, I raced down the hall toward what was essentially Stuart's hospital room, then skidded to a stop when I saw Rita standing outside it with a woman I'd never seen before.

"Oh." I forced a smile. "Rita, I'm sorry. I'd love to meet your friend, but I'm looking for Timmy, and I'm starting to get a little worried."

"Well, I'm not surprised. That boy is a fast one."

"Yes, and—"

"Why don't you take a peek into Stuart's room?"

I did, then sagged with relief when I saw him sitting at the foot of Stuart's bed with his favorite lovey, Boo Bear, beside him.

I popped my head back out before he noticed me and looked at Rita. "Thank you. Thank you so, so much."

"No problem. The little devil was almost to the top of the stairs when I noticed him. Doing well, too." She glanced around as if taking in the entire mansion. "Eddie said you were taking a lot on here. It's going to be tough keeping an eye on that one."

"Don't I know it. I don't suppose you know anyone who's into childcare?"

"Fran's always looking for extra work," she told me, referring to her daughter, who, like Rita, was in the self-defense class I'm teaching to the neighborhood women. She was also the mom of a toddler, Elena, who happened to be one of Timmy's best friends.

Still, I was regretting the question. I couldn't bring someone in who didn't know what we really do here. And I wasn't ready to share with Fran.

Hopefully someone on the housekeeping staff could be retasked. I made a mental note to ask Father Corletti as I thanked Rita for the suggestion.

"I actually wanted to introduce you to my cousin," Rita said, nodding toward the tall woman beside her. She had Rita's slender nose and small mouth. Unlike Rita, who had let herself go naturally gray, this woman's hair was a vibrant red that reminded me of Lucille Ball. But despite the color of her hair, her face made it clear that she was close in age to Rita, which put her in her late seventies or early eighties.

"It's very good to meet you, um…"

"Nancy," the redhead said.

Rita smiled brightly. "Eddie said that you were looking for a nurse to watch over Stuart, poor thing. How long has it been?"

"Almost three months. The truth is, they don't expect him to wake up."

I said the words calmly and felt proud of myself. It was starting to get easier. The hard part was that I was starting to believe it.

I drew in a breath, gathering myself.

"And Eddie said you didn't want to go the assisted living route."

"No. I really don't. Not for a lot of reasons. He needs to be here. I need to be able to watch over him." All of that was the absolute truth, even if the deeper truth was that I needed to be near him, just in case. Because if Stuart did die without waking up, there was no way I was letting a demon set up in his body.

"Well, Nancy worked as a nurse for twenty years before she got married."

"I assure you I'm more than capable of taking care of him," Nancy said. "Some people don't like this type of work, but I've seen patients that no one expected to survive wake up and walk away. Those are the moments that make it worth it," she said, as I felt a little queasy, certain she was unknowingly talking about demons. "You just never know what the universe has in store for you."

"No," I said. "You never do."

I wanted to believe this woman. I wanted to hire her on the spot. But she'd also showed up very conveniently, and I wasn't in a position to take chances.

I glanced around, thinking. "This hall is an incredibly uncomfortable place to talk," I said. "There's a small couch and a few chairs in Stuart's room. Why don't we go talk in there?" I pulled my phone out of my pocket as if I'd just gotten a text. "Give me one second, and I'll follow you."

"That sounds wonderful Kate," Rita said, then ushered her cousin into Stuart's room.

I shoved my phone back down into my pocket and pulled out the small vial of holy water that I keep in an antique perfume bottle. I started doing this recently, after Allie and I found a box of the tiny bottles at a flea market.

I realized that if I kept a few of these in my purse—and had Laura and the girls do the same—then anytime I needed to test for a demon, I could just pretend like I was going to dab some perfume on my wrist. Then I'd touch the person with my damp fingers.

They'd either think nothing of it, or they'd start to sizzle. Either way, I'd have my answer.

As I walked back into the room, I dabbed some of the liquid on my fingertips then pretended to trip on something on the floor. A lame maneuver considering the floor was pristine with no obstacles whatsoever, but I made it work.

I reached out, then grabbed Nancy's wrist with my damp hand. She gasped, and for a moment I thought *aha!* But then she said, "Oh, dear, are you okay?"

I steadied myself, then smiled at her. "Yes, sorry, I don't know what I tripped on. New shoes. Must be the flooring."

"You should watch where you're going, girlie."

49

Eddie's voice came from behind me, and I turned around to glare at him, certain he understood exactly what I'd done.

He just grinned. "I see you've met Nancy."

"You knew Rita was bringing her in?" Silently, I added that he could have warned me.

"I accidentally tripped on the poor thing, too," he said, clearly trying hard not to laugh. "Probably need to start walking with a cane."

I flashed him a smirk. "I guess we both do."

If Rita and Nancy thought our conversation was strange, they were polite enough not to show it. I rolled my eyes at Eddie, then turned back to face Rita's cousin.

"Despite my clumsiness, I truly am glad that you're here. Rita, thank you so much for arranging this. Nancy, the job doesn't pay much, but if you want it, it's yours. I'm not sure if Rita told you that it's a twenty-four hour gig, though. Basically, you'd be living in with Stuart. We have him on monitors so you can leave the room and sleep in the adjoining room, but the job is to keep an eye on him, turn him, exercise his muscles, take care of his physical needs. He's fed with an IV, but you'd need to change the bag sometimes. We do have a medical staff for the school, and they'll oversee. But you'd be the day to day care."

We'd put Stuart in the nursery attached to one of the upstairs bedrooms. My room is next door, with another attached nursery that was for Timmy. Allie was already setting up her room downstairs in the dorms. She was sharing with Mindy, and Eliza was in the room across the hall. And while Jared could have grabbed an upstairs room, he chose to take a dorm room for himself and to do dual work as a dorm monitor.

As I ran down the arrangement in my head, I realized that it was really just me up here. And for a moment, I wished that Eric had made the decision to live on property. Or Cutter. Or Laura.

Maybe I'd insist they each keep a room. For those occasions when they want to stay the night.

And, I remembered with relief, Marcus would be moving in later today. At least I wouldn't be the only conscious human on the second floor at night. Especially if Nancy took the job.

I turned my attention back to her, realizing that she hadn't answered. "Of course, if you'd rather stay at home," I added, "we could try to find someone else for another shift."

The truth was, I hadn't thought this out well at all. Then again, I wasn't expecting to find a candidate so quickly, and I was totally winging it.

"Oh, no, no. To be honest, I would love it. My Harold passed away ten years ago, and it was just me and Miss Kitty. But I lost her last year, and the house feels so very empty. Plus, the more I'm here, the more I'll see Rita. I'm sure she'll be here a lot too," she said with a significant look at Eddie.

Eddie cleared his throat, but didn't deny the comment, and I was pretty sure I saw color rise on Rita's cheeks. I thought about Stuart and hoped that we'd be just as flirtatious with each other when we were that age. Then I remembered that Stuart might not make it to that age or if he did, he might not be in any condition to flirt.

"I'm very sorry for your losses," I told Nancy sincerely.

She waved the words away. "It's a natural part of life, dear." She nodded toward Stuart's bed. "That, however, is not natural at all."

I glanced at Eddie, and he gave me the slightest shake of his head, silently telling me that he hadn't said anything to her about this being in any way a mystical injury.

"Yes," I said. "The accident was horrible."

"Rita said it was a head injury?"

"Yes. He got in the middle of a fight. Ended up getting slammed into a stone table. Banged his head pretty hard."

"I'm so sorry. There are cases though where victims came out of comas even after the doctors had lost all hope. So don't you lose hope."

I'd been told that so many times over the last few months, but for some reason, this woman saying that made me feel better. "Thank you," I said, "I promise I won't."

"I know I'll be mostly with Stuart, but I understand this school is about more than just the three Rs?"

Again, I glance at Eddie, who shrugged. "That's right," I said. "The students have an academic curriculum, of course, but the students were selected for their skills in competitive fighting. So they will be doing a lot of training. Some of them are aiming for the Olympics. Others plan to go into Hollywood stunt work."

I had no idea where that came from, but the moment I said it, I thought it made for a pretty good cover story. Something else I really should have figured out ahead of time.

And once again, I had to wonder if I could handle any of this.

"Well, I think that's lovely," Nancy said. "Kids need an outlet other than just books, books, books. When they do that, it turns into sex, sex, sex."

I'd taken a sip of water, and almost spit it out when she said that. But, honestly, I couldn't disagree. I'd never done the public school thing, but from what I'd seen on television—and what I'd seen from my own daughter and my friends' children—that was probably pretty true. If not actual sex, then definitely the thinking about it.

I turned to shoot an amused glance at Eddie and saw Eric leaning against the doorway, his expression as amused as I felt.

"Eddie, why don't you give Nancy a tour of the school," Eric suggested. "I need to speak with Kate."

"You got it," Eddie said. "Rita, I assume you're joining us?" He extended his elbow to Rita, who stood and took it. Eric and I watched as the three of them headed out of the room together. "Sounds like you got lucky," Eric said.

JULIE KENNER

"I wasn't sure about Eddie dating Rita, but I guess that just paid off. God knows I'm woefully unprepared for all of this."

"You're not. You're just inundated with details. And with the kids coming earlier, things are extra crazy."

"You got that right."

He laughed. Then the sound died as he turned his attention to Stuart. "How's he doing?" he asked, his tone somber.

"No change. I wish there was a magic wand to make him all better. And I really wish I understood what was going on with him. It's not a coma, Eric. At least not a regular one. After what happened at the hospital, I'm certain of it."

"I believe you, but that doesn't mean we're any more prepared to get him out of whatever state he's in."

I knew that, so I didn't say anything. Instead I just went to Stuart and squeezed his hand. "Can you hear me? Stuart, can you talk to me?" I waited, but nothing happened.

"He probably just doesn't want to talk around me," Eric said, his voice intentionally light. "What with the blatant male posturing."

I rolled my eyes, but inside I was grinning. Not that long ago Stuart had left me because of my demon-hunting vocation, and because Eric had moved to town.

All things considered, I probably should have told Stuart about my demon-hunting life when we first got together, or at least when Timmy was born. But I'd wanted a new start. I'd wanted him to see a Kate who didn't always have something sharp and pointy in her hands. Who wasn't always looking over her shoulder searching for the bad guy inside the stranger walking down the street.

It had been hard when he'd first learned. Then even harder when he learned that Eric had come back to life in the body of another man, a fact I'd waited far too long to share.

Ultimately, the stress and his fears about the world I lived in ripped us apart. I blame myself. I do. But a lot of it was on him as well. We weren't communicating, and he was jealous. It was all just a big mess. But the worst was when he left me and took Timmy with him. He'd said we were okay, and then he'd just flipped.

That had broken me into a million little pieces that had only been put back together when he changed his mind and joined me and Allie on our trip to Rome so that she could meet Father Corletti. Stuart's willingness to work on our marriage had been like glue. But the repair was fragile. It held together great in Italy, but once we were back, things started to shatter again, especially after Eric moved back up to San Diablo from Los Angeles to be closer to his daughter.

Stuart had gotten all weird about Eric again. But the worst was that after Allie saved the world—that wasn't the bad part—her extraordinary powers showed up in full force, Stuart started treating her differently, and that was something I couldn't forgive.

Hell, he couldn't forgive himself. He didn't want to think that way about her—at least that's what he told me —but there was a distance. A distance that, frankly, lasted until the day that he sacrificed himself to save her.

I'd like to say that grand gesture changed everything. Super glued all those cracks in our marriage and repaired that broken trust. But I don't know. I haven't had the chance to know, because I haven't had the chance to talk to him since. He's been unconscious since that horrible day when Lilith tried to get into Allie's body and Stuart foiled her. Honestly, if it weren't for Jared, Stuart would be dead. Or worse.

So now I'm in limbo. I'd told Stuart that I loved him and that our marriage was important, but that he had to understand that I loved Eric too. He had to understand that Eric was part of my life, he was Allie's father, and he was a man who I hadn't left, but who had been killed.

Eric and I had never had our ending. And, yes, now he looked different. But inside he was the same. And Stuart had told me he understood that. But we'd never had the chance to test that understanding. And now here we were, the three of us together in some brutal triangle, and I didn't have any idea how it was going to end, and I was terrified.

But I didn't actually know what it was that scared me.

Eric put his hand on my shoulder, and I jumped.

"Hey, I didn't mean to startle you. Where'd you go?"

"I don't know. I just wish ... I just wish he'd come back."

"I know."

"And I don't understand what happened the other day," I complained. "I don't understand how he spoke. I don't understand why he spoke. If it's just a regular coma, then—"

He put a finger over my lips to silence me, then he took my hand and led me out of the room. "He's going to be fine. It's going to work out."

"Do you really believe that?"

"I do. I think the fact that he said something is a good sign. I think something is starting to happen. I don't know what. I don't know if it's going to be good. I don't know if it's going to be helpful. But I know it will change things. And that's something."

"I guess...."

"You just need to go on believing that he'll be okay. That we'll all be okay. Until you know differently, that's what we all have to believe."

I nodded. We were standing outside his room now, the door open so we could keep an eye on him until Rita and Nancy got back. It probably wasn't necessary. He was hooked up to equipment that monitored him, and if anything happened to his vitals, it was wired to ring throughout the mansion.

There was also an alarm button by the door and by his bed, so that if anyone was in there with him and something should happen, they could ring it and staff would come immediately. Not just medical staff, assuming we had them, which as of yet we only have

Nancy, but also me, and anyone else who was in a position to hunt demons. Just in case.

I really didn't want to think about what the *just in case* could be, but I couldn't stop the acknowledgement that it could be a demon coming to attack Stuart. Or it could be Stuart waking up as a demon. Neither option would be pleasant, and as much as I might want to run in the other direction, the only thing I really could do was run towards Stuart and fight. That, at least, was one thing I knew how to do.

The thought triggered more angst, and I looked up at Eric. "Can I really do this? The school I mean?"

"You're asking the wrong question, Katie-kins."

I started to ask him what he meant, but I saw his expression, the way his eyes were soft on me, and I understood. I wasn't alone. I rephrased my question. "Can *we* do this?"

"Damn right we can. We are doing it."

"Their lives are in our hands. All of these kids. Allie's life."

"We know what we're doing," he said. "We were the best back in the day, and you know it."

I smiled at the arrogance in his voice. "We did make a good team." I glanced into Stuart's room, then drew in a breath. "We made a good team," I repeated. "But how much of what we were was because of what you are?"

He didn't pretend to misunderstand. He knew I was talking about the demon that had been bound inside him, put there by his parents in an abhorrent ritual.

"I don't know," he said. "That was buried deep inside

at first, remember? It only came free when we had to escape through the Cardinal Fire."

I shuddered, remembering that day. We'd been trapped, about to die at the hands of a powerful High Demon. No one survived Cardinal Fire, but Eric said that we could. And we did. Instead of killing us, the mystical fire burned away the prison in which the demonic essence inside of him had been trapped. So I suppose the demon saved us.

And that demon was also what allowed him to come back in David Long's body after he'd been killed in San Francisco. He came back just the way demons do, sliding into a human form. If it weren't for Demon Hunting, I would never have met my husband. And if it weren't for demons, he could never have come back to me.

Sometimes I think the world makes no sense at all. And sometimes I think it makes exactly the sense that it's supposed to. But that doesn't mean it's easy.

"How did our lives get so complicated?" I asked.

His grin held a lifetime of amusement. "We're Demon Hunters. What else could it be?"

I met his smile, and for a while we were just Kate and Eric.

Then he took my hands.

"Too complicated?" he asked, and I heard that extra something in his voice. Not about Demon Hunting. Not about the school. But about us.

And that's not a question I can think about, much less answer.

"Everything's complicated," I told him, pulling my hands free. "Even something as simple as who we are."

He laughed. "That's not simple."

"I was being sarcastic. And the truth is, it's getting less simple. For me, it used to be easy. I wasn't anybody."

I shrugged. That's what happens when you're an orphan wandering the streets of Rome. But recently, I began to learn about my family.

"I told you I saw the name Donnelly on Eliza's family tree."

"Have you asked her about that yet?"

"No."

I saw the surprise in his eyes. I'd seen that paper months ago. "I don't think I really want to know," I said, answering the unspoken question. "Ever since I first heard of Father Donnelly from Eddie, I've thought of him as wrong. An off priest who somehow went rogue. Maybe trying to do right, but doing it in the absolute wrong way. But now I don't know."

"What do you mean?"

"I don't know. I guess I've seen so much. Maybe he is rogue. And maybe that's bad. But maybe it's not. I hate what they did to you as a kid. But we have Allie because we survived the Cardinal Fire. And we wouldn't have survived if you weren't who Father Donnelly and your parents made you."

He shook his head slowly. "We can't go down the what-if road. You play that game and nobody ever has to take responsibility for anything."

"I guess." I closed my eyes and I rested my head

against his chest, relief flooding me as his arms pulled me close. Right then, I didn't want to think anymore. I just wanted someone to comfort me.

And as my husband lay unconscious a few feet away, I let my formerly dead husband hold me in his arms and make me feel safe.

6

About the time that Rita and Nancy returned, Marcus texted that he was fifteen minutes out in the van with the kids.

Eric signaled that he was going downstairs, but I lingered to tell Stuart what was going on. It was probably silly—I doubt he could understand what I was saying—but I went into his room and gave him a quick update anyway.

Then I kissed him lightly on the forehead, told him I loved him, and headed out of the room with a smile to Nancy, who promised to text me immediately if there was any change whatsoever in my husband's condition.

The PA system wasn't set up yet, so there wasn't a way to tell Allie that Marcus was on the way. He sent a group text, though, so I hoped that she and the others were on their way to the entrance hall. I hurried down the hall from Stuart's room toward the stairs, but when I peered over the railing, I saw only Mindy and Eliza.

"Where's Allie?" I called down. They both looked up at me, then giggled.

I got the picture.

Allie was off with Jared, and I doubted either had checked their phones.

I signaled to Laura that I was off to look for Allie, then headed to the primary training facility on the second floor. But it was completely silent. Considering their shared love for kicking and fighting and throwing knives, I didn't give up. Instead, I crossed to the back door, intending to step through it and onto the balcony to see if they were training outside.

Instead, I heard them through the partially open door.

I was hidden in the space between the window and the door, and I let their conversation wash over me, soaking in their words. I knew I should leave, but I stayed anyway.

So sue me. I'm a mom.

"You can't hold back during training," Jared said. "That's not fair to you or to us. If we're going to be a team, you have to work at full strength."

"Full strength means everyone is going to know about me."

I winced. I thought that she had come to terms with the fact that she had additional strength and speed. But that was when it was just us. Family and close friends. Now, new students were getting mixed into the game, and Allie was, despite everything, a typical teenage girl. She wanted to fit in.

63

"That's who you are," Jared said, and I wanted to high-five him.

"Yeah, but I don't have to shove it in their faces."

"If you don't train with everything you've got, then you won't have everything you've got once you're in the field. And I can't risk that. I really don't want to be staked. And beheading doesn't sound too good either. For that matter, I don't want to be captured and put into a crystal room."

I could hear the pain in his voice, and I could imagine Allie's reaction.

"Have you managed to reach her again?" Allie was asking about Celia, Jared's sister, who had been captured by Lilith's minions, then tortured and held hostage. Occasionally, Lilith had let her out of the crystal room that blocked vampire telepathy. She'd let them communicate only because she knew that his sister's fear and devolving mental health would torment Jared.

"I try every day," he said. "I've been researching crystal caves across the country, even though it feels like she's close. But most are either barely accessible or open to the public for tours. I think it's more likely a room in a house. So I've started poking around real estate sites."

"If it's a house, she probably just had her minion kill the owner," Allie said. "I doubt you'll find a listing."

"Yeah," he said. "I know. But I have to try."

"You do," she said. "I totally get it. I'd be going nuts if someone took Timmy."

Her words made my heart twist and tears prick my eyes.

"And you're right about me and my training, too," she added. "I know you are. I just want to not be a freak."

"You aren't. You're you. Anything less can get us killed."

"I know. I do. I get that it's important to go all out when we're in a fight. Because it's a matter of life or death. Or worse," she added. "Like what happened to Celia. I really am so sorry."

"Yeah, well, that's the kind of worse I don't want for you."

"I know," Allie said as I closed my eyes, wishing I could protect him from pain with the same intensity that I wished I could protect my daughter.

Soon, I was sure, I'd feel that same protective intensity for the students who'd be filling these halls.

"I just want them to like me. No, that's not even true. I just don't want them to think I'm a freak."

"You are a freak."

I heard her laugh, and it made me smile, and I pictured her pushing his shoulder. After that, there was silence, and I pictured him pulling her close.

And then, I thought, I really should leave....

I stayed.

"So you'll show them what you've got. You don't have to tell them how you got it. Maybe they'll just think you're kick-ass."

"So you're going to go all out too?"

"Sure."

"Uh-huh," she said. "And what are you going to say if they ask how you're so fast? I can't even catch up with you. Fighting, I can hold my own, but I don't have your speed."

"You're pretty close."

He was right about that. I'd seen her in that cave under Rome. Speed and agility that was increasing daily. And I imagined that she would grow into it even more.

"Stop changing the subject. Are you going to tell them that you're a vampire?"

"I guess I have to."

"Have to? Why?"

"Because we're going to be a team. They're our team-mates. We're going to be working with these kids. Training with them. And then fighting with them side by side. Besides, your mom said I have to."

She laughed. "Fair enough. Did she say why?"

"Mostly because we have to all trust each other."

"I guess. I'm just so used to secrets," she said, and I winced. I'm the one who started with the secrets.

"Yeah, well there will still be secrets, but not inside this school. Right?"

"Are we a secret?"

"Maybe. For now. But I don't want to be a secret forever."

"Me neither," she said, her voice soft.

"Good."

"But don't think you can boss me around just because you're an instructor, and we have *that* kind of secret."

I almost laughed. From her voice, I couldn't tell if she

was pissed, flirting, or petulant. I figured Jared couldn't tell either. But he rolled with it.

"Of course I can boss you around. And that's another reason I have to tell them I'm a vampire. Because if I'm going to be an instructor, I have to go all in. So since I'm supposed to be educating them on supernatural creatures, I need to tell them about myself."

"At least you're something they're familiar with, even if Hollywood mostly got it wrong."

"Yeah. I've got a jumping off point. I can either go with the classics, or sparkles, or angst. What do you think?"

She laughed. "For you, angst totally fits."

"You're going to regret you said that." I pictured him leaning closer to her as he spoke.

In my mind, she lifted her chin, staring him down. "I don't think I will."

Once again I smiled. Once again I told myself I needed to leave.

I was just about to slip away, in fact, when Allie said, "Am I one of the supernatural creatures you're going to tell them about? Me and my dad?"

"I don't know. I haven't talked to your mom or Eric about that. I was going to talk to you first. And you already know I think it should come from you."

"Do we really want to have this conversation now?" she asked

"No," Jared said. "I really don't. But I'm right," he said, his voice pitched lower.

"Maybe. Don't let it go to your head."

For a moment, there was only silence, and I took a chance and leaned back just enough so that I could peek out the window. He'd pulled her into a hug. It didn't look romantic. It looked like a friend hug. And I couldn't decide if I was pleased or disappointed.

When they pulled apart, she smirked. "I think I'll like Bruce. He sounds kick-ass. He took out that demon."

I was still watching, and I saw Jared's mouth quirk up. I wondered if she picked Bruce to mention because she really was impressed by what he did in saving the other students, or if she saw him as a possible foil to make Jared jealous. I hoped she wasn't playing those kind of games, but I had to admit I wouldn't be surprised. Still, with over a hundred years under his belt, I had a feeling Jared had seen every dating game in the book.

"I imagine he'll like you, too," Jared said.

"At least until I beat him. He's probably used to always winning. To getting the drop on everyone. One round with me, and he might not be so happy to be my friend after all."

"He will. Once he gets to know you. And don't judge people too harshly. Not everyone sees the world in black and white, better and worse. They'll see all your good qualities, and you'll see theirs."

"Sometimes it's annoying that you're so much older than me. You sound like an adult."

He laughed. "I'll try to do better."

"Thank you."

"They're going to think of you in the same way.

They'll think you're a freak. You'll have to show them differently, too."

"Yeah, well I think I can. I haven't had human blood in forever, so I won't be scary to them. Glowering at their necks with pulsing veins."

He said the words, and I knew he meant them, but I was still nervous. He'd told us that he'd been drinking only animal blood for several years. I hoped that was true. Because if he'd been drinking human blood, he was dangerous. Especially when he was fighting.

I realized they'd been talking while my mind wandered, and once again I told myself I needed to leave. Once again, I didn't. Instead I stayed and listened.

"Allie..."

"What?"

"Never mind." His voice was soft. I'd heard that tone before.

"What?" She repeated, but this time her tone was soft, too.

"You know what. But I'm one hundred and twelve years older than you."

"Yeah, but you never stopped hell from busting out all over with your blood." I heard the tease in her voice. A kind of sensual hum. "So I'm thinking there's something pretty ancient inside me. Like maybe a thousand years ancient. Which means I win."

I realized I was smiling. In fights and in romance, my kid could hold her own. And I was a terrible mother for not leaving, but I told myself the floorboards might creak. So better to just stay perfectly still.

"So if you win, what's your prize?"

"I— Oh hell, you are," she said, and right then, I knew I had to l go. They deserved privacy. But at the same time, I was terrified that this was the moment when Jared would break my daughter's heart, and she'd need me.

But if so, I had to trust that she'd find me, and I had to force myself to walk away now.

Like it or not, she was growing up and finding her own path. It was both bittersweet and poignant knowing that her path led away from me. But what kept me sane was knowing that same road would always lead her home.

7

"We're here," Marcus called, striding through the double front doors that we'd opened wide. Now the van was parked on the circular drive and the students were piling out of the side doors.

The gate was locked behind the van, and the house-keeping staff was already out there, unloading luggage onto carts that they'd wheel to the former servants' wing that now serves as the dorm and recreation room area. Each student had already been assigned a room and a roommate, and if the staff did their job right, each kid would leave the welcome meeting to find their room with their belongings at the foot of their bed.

After that, the plan was dinner—pizza since we were still short a kitchen team—and a movie in the theater. Because how can teens move into a house that has an actual theater and not use it right off the bat? We hadn't decided what to watch yet, but I planned to do a search for spooky movies set in boarding schools. Allie's suggestion, and I thought it was a good one.

Moving forward, Marcus and Cutter would be using the theater for reviewing training tapes, a plan that I was one hundred percent behind. So long as we still got to have movie night every now and then.

Right then, though, it was time for introductions, which meant that I was soon to be on deck, and I stood on the fourth step of the grand staircase so that I'd have a bit of height over the rest of them.

The first to follow Marcus in was a tall, wiry girl with short hair, no make-up, and huge brown eyes—which I only caught a glimpse of in the two seconds that she looked up from the floor. She was wearing a tank top under overalls and slouched into the room. She had to be Ana, as Jessica had killed Dani, the only other girl in the group. I knew from her profile that she was fourteen and had gotten noticed by *Forza* scouts when she'd successfully fought off a hellhound.

Not an easy feat, as I well knew.

She took a spot a few feet away from where Mindy and Eliza stood, the only students in the room. I frowned, thinking that I should have interrupted Jared and Allie after all. And that they'd be getting a rude interruption any minute, because I was about to send Eddie after them.

"We're here, we're here!" Allie's shout came from behind me, and she and Jared hurried into the room. He met my eyes, his apologetic. Mine, I'm sure, were cold.

Allie had an excuse, albeit a crappy one. She was a student.

But Jared was an instructor. He should know better. He winced, mouthed *sorry,* and moved to stand by Eric and the rest of the instructors.

I tried to catch Allie's eyes, but she was purposefully avoiding mine as she slid in beside Ana.

The next kid to settle into a spot was Ren, a fifteen-year-old Chinese American from Manhattan whose parents had been killed in a demon attack when he was only six. The scouts had kept an eye on him over the years, and when he successfully managed living on the streets after running away from his foster home, they offered him a place at a shelter while quietly assessing his potential as a Hunter.

He wore baggy jeans and an oversized tee that swallowed his slight, but clearly agile body. His close-cropped hair accentuated his eyes and easy smile. A little too easy, as I think it covered nerves. Then again, under the circumstances, who wouldn't be nervous?

The last to enter was Bruce, who strode in like he owned the place. Tall, blond, and athletic, he looked like the solid fighter the scouts had reported him to be, and he'd proven himself by taking out the Jessica demon, but I worried about his ability to play well with others, especially after reading about his series of foster homes and history of disciplinary problems.

Hunters tended to be loners, so if I was right, it wouldn't be a huge problem. But at the same time, the students at this school needed to be able to trust each other and follow instructions. He'd been noticed after a hot-tempered Hunter had taken him on after Bruce had inadvertently let a demon get away.

So there they were, only three candidates. Even five was a small number, and I knew that it was getting harder and harder to recruit Demon Hunters. I hoped we could find the eighteen I was shooting for next semester, but I wasn't optimistic. Father Corletti once told me that kids don't have the interest anymore. They're used to video games and digital demons. They don't want to truly get down and dirty. And most of them don't believe the world is worth saving.

Considering what had happened to our new recruits in their young lives, I kind of understood where they were coming from.

"What now?" Bruce said. "We're here."

"Thanks to you," I said with a welcoming smile. "You did excellent work in Tulsa."

His brow furrowed, as if he wasn't sure if I was being sarcastic or not. I reminded myself that these kids had lived mostly on the street. Trust came hard. Finally, he shrugged. "I know my stuff."

"You proved that. After you graduate from here, you'll know even more stuff. All of you will," I said, looking out at the group. "I'm not going to make you all share your life stories, but I do hope you spend some time after the movie getting to know each other."

"Movie?" Ren asked.

"That is the plan," I confirmed. "Pizza and a movie. But let me back up. I'm Kate Connor, and I'm a Level

Six Demon-Hunter with *Forza Scura*, which, as you know is a secret arm of the Vatican. First rule of *Forza*, don't talk about *Forza.*"

As I hoped, they all laughed, though whether any of them actually got the movie reference was anyone's guess.

I went around the room next, first introducing Eric and describing how we used to hunt together. "He'll be helping out when needed in the training room, and teaching you history, lore, all that juicy book-learning stuff that most of us don't care about because we just want to fight."

Once again, they laughed. So far, this was going okay. Then again, it was day one, minute one, and I expected them to be on their best behavior. Too soon to call myself a raging success.

They'd already met Marcus, but I gave a bit more information about his time at the Vatican and his legendary father who'd trained both me and Eric. I introduced Cutter as a trainer and Laura as their research guru. Then I moved on to the other students, starting with Jared since he straddled student and teacher.

"You're shitting us," Ana said when he told them he was a vampire.

"I assure you, he's not," I said.

"But don't worry. I won't turn into a bat or bite you." Jared smiled sweetly. "Unless you piss me off."

"But aren't you, like, you know ... a demon?" Ana winced, as if embarrassed to ask the question.

"You mean like on TV? Body dies, memories stay,

otherwise a demon moves in? And, honestly, how does that work? The memories just hang around?"

The kids all looked at each other, then shrugged.

"No," Jared said. "A demon didn't slide into me when I was turned. The only thing demonic is in my family tree. The original dude thousands of years ago who managed to turn himself into a vampire after slicing the neck of another guy and then drinking his blood. *That* other guy was a demon. Otherwise, all me with all my memories. And, yeah, I'm young enough I can still walk in the sun."

Three hands shot up.

"You can ask more later," I said. "Jared will be helping out in fight training and also instructing you on supernatural creatures so plenty of time for questions. And, of course, there's Eddie."

I gestured to Eddie, who shuffled forward, putting the old man show on thick.

Bruce snickered.

"Think you could take me?" Eddie asked.

Bruce looked at his two companions, his expression clear enough—*Is that a trick question?*

"Come on, then, boy."

Bruce looked at me, and I nodded.

"Okay, old man," he said, then rushed forward. As he did, Eddie got him with a low-level taser blast, and Bruce fell shaking to the ground.

"What the hell?" His voice was weak at first, then stronger as he climbed to his feet after the shock wore off. "What the hell was that?"

"That was a reminder that even demons have access to technology. Take nothing for granted."

"Eddie's been around longer than any of us," I said. "And he knows more than any of you, I promise. The man's an asset and a resource. Learn from him."

Bruce crossed his arms, and stayed surly, but I couldn't blame him. Ren and Ana looked intrigued, and I hoped they'd seek Eddie out. Not only because I truly believed that they'd learn, but because I wanted Eddie to have an excuse to come here daily. Already, I missed having him around.

I let the students introduce themselves next, starting with Mindy. "Yeah, so, that's my mom, Ms. Dupont. And I'm here to study to be an *alimentatore.*"

"Not a Hunter?" Ren asked.

Mindy shook her head. "I like the book stuff. But I've killed demons before," she said. "It's pretty cool."

"*Very* cool," Eliza said, then gave her name. "I'm Kate —I mean, Ms. Connor's—cousin, and my mom hunted demons, too. Just not for *Forza*. I guess you'd call her freelance. But I want into that fight, and I want to live, too. So I'm glad that *Forza* opened this school and that Kate—Ms. Connor—is running it. She's freaking awesome."

"Thanks, Eliza."

"Just calling it as I see it. And that's Allie. Her daughter," she added. "Well, their daughter," she amended, pointing to Eric, who was making a show of leaning on his cane. She winced. "Was I supposed to say that?"

"It's fine," Eric told her. "No secrets among Hunters, right?"

"You're the one who came back," Bruce said, looking at Eric. "When I was living with the Hunter who hooked me up with you guys, he told me a story. You were like kick-ass when you were young. And you got married. And you had her," he said, pointing to Allie.

"Right," Ana said. "I heard that, too. You retired. And then you got mugged and died. But you came back." She took a step back, shaking her head. "That is seriously freaky."

"So you're their daughter?" Ren said, turning toward Allie, but pointing to me and Eric. "Wow."

"That means you're the one," Bruce said to Allie. "You like closed the gates to hell. You saved the freaking world."

"No way," Ana said.

"Oh, yeah," Bruce said. "Beautiful and kick ass."

I watched as Allie's cheeks turned red, and Jared took a step closer. "Gee." Allie shifted her weight. "Didn't realize anyone actually knew about that."

"Like I said. That Hunter who turned *Forza* on to me. He knew."

I frowned, wondering how he could have heard. Allie was right. What happened to Eric had become well known within *Forza*. But Father Corletti had made great efforts to keep who Allie was a secret exactly for this reason. She didn't want the eyes on her, or the inevitable questions about what made her special.

Apparently the secret wasn't a well-kept one.

"What was that Hunter's name?" Eric asked.

"Jonathan Bartlett."

"Bartlett's dead," Eric said.

I wanted to call him out for being an insensitive ass. After all, that Hunter was Bruce's friend. But then I realized he did it on purpose. The fact was, it was humans who didn't know Allie's secret. But many actual demons *did* know. And Eric was making sure that Bruce wasn't working with them.

Bruce took a step back, his head shaking and his expression one of total shock. "No. No way. What happened—Oh, God. Was it a demon?"

Eric nodded, and I saw tears in Bruce's eyes as he turned to the two he'd arrived with. "He—he's the reason we're alive. The reason I knew what to do. Though the eye, I mean." He shook himself, then took a few deep breaths before lifting his chin. "I'm in. If I hadn't said it before, I am so in."

"Good." I looked to the other two. "This is your final chance to say no. Tomorrow, your education starts."

"I'm in, too," Ren said

"Yeah," Ana agreed. "Totally in."

Then all the kids started talking at once, and I held up a hand to quiet them, but to no avail.

Finally, Eric whistled, and the room went still.

"In a few moments, you'll be shown to your rooms so you can settle. You all have a binder on your bed with your schedule. You're our first class, so you're small, and we want your feedback. Next semester will be much more crowded and much more scheduled.

"How long are we here?" Ana asked.

"Until you crash and burn or until we think you're ready to go out into the world."

"Hey, I'm ready now," Bruce said.

"You might be ready on the fighting side," I told him, though I doubted it. I had a feeling he could do with a take down from Cutter. "But you also need the knowledge that goes with being a Hunter. So there will be book learning, too. I know," I added in response to their groans. "It's not my thing, either."

"We'll start out training and studying," Eric said.

"When do we get to fight?" Bruce asked.

"Maybe tomorrow. We'll check the news, see where there might be some newly made demons."

"Seriously?" Ren said.

"No better way to learn than in the fight," he said. "And San Diablo has a High Demon population, so it's a good place to get your feet wet."

"That's so cool. And we really live here?" Ana asked. "For free? And you feed us, too?"

"So long as you're in the Academy, yes. That means you're doing the work and improving. Got it?"

They all nodded, including Allie, Mindy, and Eliza.

I went over the list of who lived on site, and explained that we were still short-staffed. "The kitchen help won't arrive for another few days, but we do have housekeeping —that doesn't mean you get to trash your rooms—and there's a maintenance team if you have any problems with computers, plumbing, lights, anything. For help with weapons, access to training rooms or the rare book section of the library after hours, you see an instructor. Got it?"

Again, they nodded, and I was starting to be a little bit proud of myself. This headmistress thing was going okay.

"Everyone follow Laura," I continued. "She's going to give you the tour and end at the dorms. You'll have to decide among yourselves who gets which bed."

I turned and saw one of the furniture assembly guys standing a few yards behind me with a clipboard. A supervisor, I assumed, and I frowned, realizing I should have put someone with them to prevent this kind of wandering. But if he overheard anything he considered odd, it wasn't showing on his face.

"Perfect timing," I told the kids, with a nod toward the supervisor. "Looks like your desks are all assembled, right?"

The supervisor nodded, and I headed over to sign, only to spring backward when he lashed out with the clipboard, the sharp, metal edge slicing only inches from my throat. "Bitch!" he howled. "You think you can increase their numbers? We shall cut them all down."

"The hell you will," I growled as I steadied myself, spun around, and used the momentum to plant a serious kick right in the middle of his chest.

He stumbled, then fell flat on his back. I leaped on him, immediately smelled his rotten, demon breath, then realized I had no weapon.

I grimaced, but decided what the hell, then jammed

my forefinger right into his eye socket. Good lesson for the students, right?

Immediately, the air shimmered as the demon left the body to fade back into the ether.

Done.

Except not so much. Because when I turned, I saw the full furniture assembly crew burst out from the corridor that led to the dorms. At least a dozen, and every last one of them was looking for blood.

8

"Allie!" I called. "Behind you!"

She whipped around in time to see a pony-tailed assembly worker toss Ren to the ground. "Jared! Knife!"

He threw it, and she caught and redirected it so fast I could barely make out the movements. But the end result was clear enough—the knife went straight through the demon's eye, and in that moment, it went limp, dropping Ren, who was sprawled on the floor, his eyes wide with awe.

"Get up," Allie shouted, running to take his hand. I headed that way, too, passing Marcus, who landed a blow on a demon who was barreling toward Ana, and knocking him off course.

"Got him," Eric said, pulling the sword from his cane and stabbing the diverted demon in the eye.

Across the room, three demons were converging on Mindy, who had taken off her jacket and was using it as a flail. Jared practically flew to her side, then pulled her out of their converging circle as Allie swooped in and—with one graceful move—used the sword Eric tossed her to spin in a circle and remove three heads in one efficient maneuver.

"Gramps!" she called to Eddie, but Bruce was already hurrying to his side. Eddie waved him off. "I've got it, I've got it," he said, then proved his point by shoving his favorite stiletto deep into the beast's eye.

As for me, I was cursing myself for not having my favorite stiletto on me. Usually, it was always at my side, but I guess being at the academy had given me a false sense of security.

Never again.

I assessed the situation, then saw a demon getting past Cutter, who was holding off a cluster of demons snarling at Laura.

"He's heading for Stuart!" I called. I was still on the far side of the room, but there was no one else who wasn't already wrestling a demon. Even Bruce was fighting alongside Ana and Ren.

Cursing and terrified, I raced that way, certain this must be all about Stuart, and knowing with absolute certainty that neither Nancy nor Rita were any match for the demon. Not even with the taser I knew Rita kept in her purse.

But I shouldn't have worried. I heard the howls behind me, and paused just long enough to look over my shoulder. I gasped at the slaughter I saw. A room full of dead demons, and my daughter looking triumphant as she used Jared's knife to take down the last one that had turned its attention on Eliza.

A moment later, Allie had retrieved the knife and was sending it flying toward the demon on the stairs. Its back was to her, but the knife lodged in its neck, making it stumble. It growled, then turned—and Allie was right there, having practically flown past me to the demon's side, even managing to catch the stiletto that Eddie tossed her in the process.

She used the knife to impale the demon. It howled, then collapsed, and everyone in the room turned and looked at Allie.

She shrugged, looking sheepish. "What? I've been training, okay?"

"I guess so," Ren said, awe in his voice.

"Holy crap," Ana added. "If I can learn to do even half that, that would be seriously cool."

"Yeah, well, we'll work on it," Allie said, her eyes finding Mindy, who shot her two thumbs up.

"So, um, dorms? Want me to lead the way?"

"Great idea," I told her. "We'll get this cleaned up, then text you when we're ready for pizza and the movie." I turned my attention to Mindy. "Get everyone on a group text, okay?"

"Sure thing," she said, as if this was just another day. Honestly, it pretty much was. Another demon attacking our home. Another battle to fight it back.

What's that saying about familiarity breeding contempt? I'm pretty sure it applied to demons.

"Um, excuse me?" Ana's hand went into the air.

"Yes?"

"How are you going to clean that up?" She nodded at the pile of demon carcasses.

I met Eric's eyes. "That's a lesson for another day. Trust me. Not before pizza."

Ana nodded, then turned quickly away. Allie shot me a grin, then she and Eliza took the lead as they headed toward the dorms. Mindy hung back, then raced to Laura for a hug. "Love you, Mom."

"You, too, baby," she said, before Mindy hurried to catch up. "Can we please not do that again," Laura said once Mindy was out of earshot.

"I'll second that," I said, and the others nodded.

Nobody moved toward a body. Not that I blamed them. I wasn't moving either.

"Looks like Bruce will be an asset," Laura said.

Cutter shrugged. "Seems a little arrogant."

"So are you," Laura teased.

I laughed. "Score one for the girls' team."

"I'm siding with Cutter," Marcus said. "And I'm the one who spent a cross-country drive with the kid."

"Arrogance can be an asset," Eric said. "Especially if he gets taken down a peg. Might make him fight harder to get back on top."

"Did he get taken down a peg today?" Marcus asked. "Because arrogant or not, he held the line. Not bad for a first day."

"Can't argue with that," I said.

"Eh, the whole batch seems okay," Eddie said. "But none of them's got what our girl has."

"That's true enough," Cutter said. "I've been training her for years, and I don't have a clue where she picked up some of those moves. I mean, other than from you, Eric, and I'm still not sure how that worked."

"You and me both," Eric said. "But I'm proof that it did. Or Allie is."

"Poor kid," Marcus says.

Eddie shook his head. "No. That kid's special. She's got a gift. And she can handle it. Poor Allie? Not hardly. Poor demons sounds a lot more likely."

I reached out and squeezed Eddie's hand. "Exactly," I said to him. Then I looked at each of them in turn. "Did anybody notice anything about her?" I asked.

"Notice?" Cutter frowned. "You mean her moves. I already told you I was amazed how advanced she's gotten."

"No. Not that. Did you notice how the demons were with her?"

For a moment, they were all silent. Then Eric nodded. "I did. I hoped I was wrong."

"You weren't," I told him.

"What?" Laura asked.

"The demons weren't attacking her," I said.

"Don't be ridiculous. Of course they—*oh*."

"Damn," Cutter said. "You're right."

"And Allie? Did our girl realize she was getting the royal treatment?" Eddie's scowl was severe. I couldn't blame him.

"That's the million dollar question," Eric said.

I shook my head. "No, the million dollar question is why. Why on earth would they leave her alone?"

I met Eric's eyes, terrified of what this meant. "It's not that they're scared of her."

"No," Eric agreed. "It's not."

I closed my eyes and drew a breath. "It's because of what she is. Of what she can do."

"Lilith," Laura said. "You're talking about her hosting Lilith."

"Honestly, I don't know," Eric said. "But they must want her for something. Why else keep her alive? Why else not even try to take her out?"

I leaned against Eric, feeling suddenly cold. Laura's eyes met mine, hers full of sympathy. "It's never going to end, is it? Her being what she is? Standing out? Being talked about?"

No one answered. I didn't expect them to. It wasn't really a question, after all.

"Well, there is one good thing," Eric said.

I tilted my head to look at him. "Yeah?"

"Father Donnelly's in town, but he didn't come by."

"Yeah," I agreed. "That's definitely one good thing."

9

I leaped back, my arm stinging from the unexpected assault, then steadied myself and glared at the hot, bubbling chaos in front of me. The pale white faces. The gooey yellow eyes that seemed to be laughing at me. That overpowering scent of burning oil accompanied by snapping and popping.

I had no one to blame but myself. I knew that. I'd gotten myself into this mess, and I didn't have a single clue what to do now.

"Just flip them," Laura said from behind me.

"They're cooking too fast," I retorted, thrusting my hand with the spatula closer as I winced in anticipation of another drop of oil splattering against my arm.

I slid the spatula gently under one, lifted, then flipped. The yolk broke, and half the egg ended up outside of the frying pan. I sighed, once again defeated by domesticity.

Frankly, that was more or less par for the course as far

as me and cooking were concerned. But considering I had mouths to feed, knowing that the status quo was still intact didn't make me feel better.

"Why the hell did I think eggs for breakfast would be a good idea, anyway?"

"I told you to go with scrambled."

"Fine, fine. You were right. This is why I need you living on site." I'd called her at dawn to beg her to come to the school early. "I need to feed the masses," I'd said, "and I haven't got a clue."

She'd scored major bestie points by not even complaining. Just yanked her hair into a ponytail, thrown on jeans, and raced over here. We'd decided on eggs, but I'd insisted on fried and scrambled, just to make sure all the kids were happy.

My bad.

"Fix it?" I begged meekly, passing her the spatula.

She grimaced but took it, then expertly flipped the remaining eggs, only to discover they were all burned on the bottom.

I blew out a noisy breath. Seriously, fighting a demonic horde was less stressful than this.

"So why exactly don't we have a cook?" Laura asked.

I raised my hands as if in defeat. "We will. But then the kids came early, and..." I trailed off with a scowl.

"I've got your back until then," she assured me. "I'm thinking lots of Pop-Tarts and microwave bacon. And now I'm pulling kitchen rank. No argument." She stared me down, waiting until I nodded in meek agreement and said, "We're starting over with scrambled."

"And that," I said as she headed to the giant fridge, "is why I love you."

"Except that we're out of eggs."

I blew a raspberry as I exhaled, then met Laura's eyes. "Cereal?" we said in unison, then laughed.

"Oh, God, check for milk," I said. "I don't want to get our hopes up."

She waved a hand at the interior of the fridge, well-stocked despite the shortage of eggs.

"Look at us," she said. "Feeding an entire school. We are amazing."

"Oh, yeah, we are," I said as we took the cereal boxes and cartons of milk to one of the huge tables that dominated the dining room. Then I went to the system control panel that *Forza's* tech team had installed and pressed the button to announce breakfast. I'd already sent the wake-up alarm before I started the Great Egg Debacle, so I expected a horde of kids any moment now.

Sure enough, I heard the clatter of feet pounding down the corridor, then squeals of appreciation at the breakfast selection. Apparently, cereal was a big hit.

"We nailed it," I said, pouring a cup of coffee and adding more cream than a human needed. I deserved it.

We both took a moment to hug our girls, then headed out to let the students get to know each other on their own. To be honest, I wanted to linger and listen—they were once again reliving last night's battle, going over each of their attacks and victories—but Laura urged me away.

"She'll be fine. Even if they comment on the fact that

she did most of the fighting, Allie's going to be fine. Mindy and Eliza have her back, right? Jared, too."

I forced a nod, taking one last glance before she dragged me forcibly from the doorway. The last thing I saw was Bruce sliding into the empty seat to Allie's left with a smile that was more than a little flirtatious—and Jared's dark scowl aimed right at the back of the boy's head.

I'd already left Timmy with Marcus in the main training center before the cooking fiasco began, so Laura and I headed up the stairs so I could retrieve my little guy before going to check on Stuart.

We were midway up the grand staircase when Laura paused, drawing a deep breath. "As much as I've been working out with you, you'd think these stairs were worse than an hour on the elliptical."

"Well, it is a lotta stairs," I said. "And I'm guessing you didn't get much sleep last night, what with Mindy moving out. And I don't mean in the sad and lonely insomnia sort of way," I added, thinking of Cutter as I flashed a lascivious grin.

"Yeah," she said. "I hardly slept a wink with my little girl gone. Poor, poor me."

We shared a laugh before my melancholy took over. I had no one to worry with now. No one to share the fun kind of insomnia with. Stuart had been taken from me —*please, God, temporarily*—and Eric was very much off limits.

And, yeah, sure, Timmy made a great snuggle companion, but it really wasn't the same.

I pushed off the mood and continued up the stairs. "Just don't distract him too much during the day," I teased. "The man's here to train."

"Hey, professional here. I'm going to say hi, then go get settled in the admin office. I know you're jealous," she added. "I'm expecting a full day of paperwork." Stuart had been handling all the administrative stuff that went with opening a private school. Fortunately, he'd asked for help early on, and Laura had volunteered. For the last few months, she'd picked up where he left off, and I was left blissfully unaware of everything that had to happen behind the scenes.

"Have I mentioned how much I love that you're working here?"

"Have I mentioned how glad I am that I can?"

I returned her grin, but my smile faded quickly as we reached the landing. "What?" she asked. "I can practically hear you thinking."

I stopped, turning to face her. "There must be another chalice stone."

"Please tell me you changed the subject and that I'm not supposed to have filed some sort of order form for one of those things."

"No, no, I'm being serious. We said it last night, right? Lilith must be planning another attempt at getting inside Allie. But to do that, she'd need another chalice stone. All we need to do is find it and break it."

She moved to lean against the ornate handrail as I paced in front of her, my sneakers silent on the tile flooring. "It's a good theory, Kate, except it doesn't pan out."

I came to a stop, my attention fully on my friend. "Of course it does. It's the only explanation."

"Except that I've now read everything in the universe about that chalice. Which, considering it turned out to be a stone table, was very poorly named."

"And?"

"And it was one of a kind. Now that it's broken, she can't recreate that ritual."

I shook my head. "No. That can't be right. She isn't asking her demonic minions to hold off out of respect for my daughter. You must have missed it."

She tilted her head and stared me down. "One, I'm getting pretty good at research. Two, it wasn't just me. It was me and Eric and Eddie all looking. Plus Mindy, who has really got a knack for this. And, just to add extra icing to the cake, Father Corletti also assigned a team to research."

"How come I didn't know any of this?"

She widened her eyes, but otherwise didn't answer.

"Right. Duh. I get it. But it doesn't make sense."

"Not a lick of sense," Laura agreed. "Honestly, we all thought it was great news, but after yesterday all I can think is that—"

"There must be another ritual," I said, finishing the thought. "Well, damn."

"There are some ancient tablets that talk about lost rituals that honored Lilith. My new plan is to scour them."

"Yes," I said. "Good plan. Maybe there's some ritual to bind her to a human. Or to force a human to consent to time-sharing." Lilith couldn't move in uninvited, but I knew first hand that she was willing to lower herself to share a body. She'd shared with that bitch Nadia, after all, and I'd almost lost Eric all over again, not to mention Allie. In the end, we'd all survived, but Eric had lost an eye in the battle.

We'd defeated Lilith, though, and I needed to keep remembering that. We'd done it once, we could do it again.

"Anything you can find," I urged Laura. "No matter how improbable. "She's regrouping. We need to be prepared."

We started walking toward the training center. We were close enough to hear the *oofs* and *thuds* when Laura stopped again.

"She doesn't know what the ritual is either," Laura said, her words coming slowly, as if the thought was just starting to make sense to her.

"Why do you say that?

"Because if she had one, she'd have had her minions try to take Allie. To get her away. Imprison her so she'd be handy."

"But if she doesn't have the ritual, she's not going to risk it. Not yet. We might track Allie down before she's ready. Mess up some essential component."

"She's searching too," I said, then grinned. "And we're going to win."

"Pressure," Laura said. "I need to remember that I work well under pressure."

"You do," I assured her as we starting walking again.

95

Relief flowed through me. Not the big, robust kind. But a little thread of relief that accompanied a small victory. Eventually, of course, Lilith would come up with a solution. Demons were pesky that way. But until then ... well, until then my little girl had an invisible force field against demons.

A supernatural Get Out of Jail Free card.

At that, at least, was a tiny bit of good news.

We found Cutter and Marcus already in the training room with Allie and Mindy. "She's looking really good," I told Laura as we stood in the doorway watching the girls train. "Mindy, I mean."

"I know. I'm terrified she's going to want to switch from books to fighting." She glanced sideways at me and shrugged. "Sorry, but I am."

"I get it. Even with her skills coming along the way they are, I still get it. I mean, I almost wish that Allie wanted to go the *alimentatore* route."

I looked again at my daughter, knowing that wasn't possible. Her path had been chosen for her. "She's getting better every day," I said. "Exponentially better."

"You're worried."

"On the one hand, I'm not," I told her. "Gives me a nice, warm fuzzy feeling knowing that she can take care of herself."

"But...?"

I shrugged as I watched my daughter, my eyes on Allie as I spoke to Laura. "I'm afraid she's going to get cocky."

"Yeah, I get that. I'm afraid for that, too. With Allie, I mean. Mindy might get cocky, but I doubt it."

We both laughed. Mindy was about as uncocky as they came.

"Kate..."

"What?" I could hear the heaviness in her voice. "Is something wrong?"

"No." She shook her head, her forehead creasing. "No, not wrong, just ... just after yesterday ... I ... I don't know. I'm scared. About the school. For these kids."

"I know. Me, too. Yesterday was scary."

"It was more than scary," Laura said. "Demons were right here. In the school. And we actually invited them in."

"We did. And Eric and I have already talked about that." We'd talked late into the night, in fact. Although before the talk there had been tears. And he'd held me and told me that we were still learning, just like the students. That I had this.

That *we* had this.

And then I'd made him leave, because honestly, I liked the sound of *we* a little too much. I was relying on him, which would be fine if he was just another administrator. But he was my ex-husband. A man I still loved, and who I knew loved me.

But my current husband was right there, needing me. And though I'd spent the last several months letting Eric prop me up, I couldn't allow myself to take it a step further and cling to him. I couldn't use him to make everything feel better, not even for a moment. Not like that.

No matter how much I wanted to.

I shook the memory off, one I'd already forced deep, deep down. And now, down it went again, into the trash pile of Very Bad Cravings.

"Yesterday was my mistake," I said to Laura, telling myself that I was only talking about the furniture assembly team. "We didn't properly vet, and we let them in close. That was on me. I should have vetted the team better. I should have realized that the demon population wasn't going to want a demon fighting academy right herein San Diablo. Of course they were going to send in demons to try to take us out."

"How do you vet for something like that?"

I shrugged. "Working on it. But I'm thinking we need a holy water basin or something at the entrance. Wash your hands before entering."

Laura laughed, but the sound was thin. I studied my friend. "Are you thinking about pulling Mindy out? Making her live at home?"

Allie would be devastated if Mindy was no longer her roommate. And even more devastated if Mindy dropped out of the program altogether.

Laura hesitated, then shook her head. "No. No she belongs here. But I thought about it." She doesn't meet my eyes, and I wait, giving her time before she continues. "I spent all of last night thinking about it."

"*All* of last night?"

As I'd hoped, she grinned. "Slight exaggeration. And, I thought about it a lot. Keeping her at home. Sending her back to Coronado High. Hell, I even thought about moving. Just getting away from all this."

She looked at me and I saw guilt in her eyes, and it felt like a stab to the gut.

"Do you think I'd blame you for that?"

She shook her head. "No. I thought I'd blame me."

I tilted my head, my brow furrowed with an unspoken question.

"It's just that I can't unknow it," Laura said.

I let her words sink in, nodding slowly. "Yeah. I get that. Boy do I get that."

"I really did think I could simply walk away. I mean, you did, right? But that was different. You'd already lived a lifetime of demon hunting when you retired. You and Eric had earned your way out. Plus, you moved some place where you didn't think that you would have to fight demons. Because I know both of you. If there were demons, you'd fight, even if you were retired."

Also true. San Diablo was supposed to be a demon-free zone, and for a while it was. Then things changed, and here we were.

"You and Eric did your part to save the world," Laura said, "and then you stopped. "But you're back in now. Not because you have to be, maybe not even because you want to be, but because it's what you have to do. Because you've seen the way the world really is."

I stayed silent, letting her words flow over me. Her

words reflected my journey, but I knew she was talking about hers.

"I didn't used to see that world," Laura said. "The dark world that you've known since you were little. But I see it now, and I can't walk away from it. We live in a world with horrible things in it. But there are good things too. And since I see that, since I know it, I have to help." She let her shoulders rise and fall. "I just wish I could help more."

"You help tons," I said, realizing that my lashes were damp with tears. " And honestly, sometimes I'm sorry I showed it to you. It is horrible, knowing what we know. It changes everything. But at the same time, I'm not sorry at all. I like that you're beside me. And I can't tell you what a relief it was to stop keeping secrets from my best friend."

"Yeah, I'm glad too. But you didn't exactly show me, remember? I kind of stuck my nose in."

I laughed. She'd followed me, seen me stab a man through the eye, and pretty much freaked out. Who wouldn't? I could have made up a story, though I still don't know exactly what that story would have been, but I didn't want to.

"I'm glad you didn't," she said when I told her all that. "I wouldn't go back even if I could, and I won't pull Mindy out even though I'm scared. No from the school or the dorms."

"And you...?"

She laughed. "I am not selling my house to move in

here. At least not yet. And definitely not until you have a full-time cook," she added with a wink.

I pointed vaguely in the direction of the library downstairs. "Go. Research."

"Admin first. After that, today's all about researching ways that Lilith could get into Allie. I'll text Eric and have him meet me, and get him and Eddie on it, too."

"Good. The more the merrier."

"I'm still not familiar with Eric's library—have you seen all the books he had hauled in and set up in there? Some of those books are incredible. And scarily ancient. But I don't know how to read half of them, and I'm afraid to turn the pages on the others. And the *Forza* database is still a mystery to me. I'll get there, but boy do I have a steep learning curve."

"That's what you get for not taking ancient Sumerian in college."

"What can I say? I was a slacker."

"In the meantime, there's always Google."

In our early days fighting demons in San Diablo, Laura's internet searching skills had given the *Forza* data-base a run for its money. "The good old days," she said. "I remember when all the bad guys wanted from Allie was to impregnate her with demon spawn."

"Don't even joke about that," I said, but at the same time I had to agree with Laura.

Her brow furrowed. "Can Jared have kids?"

"Laura!"

"I'm not suggesting *that*. I'm just curious."

"I cannot even go there. That is not allowed in my brain."

"You don't know the answer."

I tilted my head and stared her down. "And that surprises you?" Laura knows perfectly well that research and the nitty-gritty factual part of this business were not my forte.

She snorted. "No, it really doesn't." She started to step away. "I'm off to research. Are you going to train with them?"

"No. Lucky me, I have administrative things to do, too. I'm not really sure why I took this job," I added, only half-kidding.

She flashed me a final grin and continued down the hall, passing Ana who was sporting baggy sweats with a T-shirt that was at least two sizes too big, leaving her looking like she had no form at all.

She paused in the doorway beside me. "Hey."

"Good morning, Ana. Did you sleep okay after last night?"

She lifted a shoulder. "Took a while to fall asleep. But no nightmares. Eliza says it'll get easier. The falling asleep part."

"So you guys are getting along? Good roomie match?"

"I guess. She's nice. Probably hated getting stuck with me."

"I doubt that."

Once more, she shrugged, then ran her hand over her close-cropped hair. Her skin was the color of dark caramel, and I remembered that her dossier indicated that her mother was black and her father was born in Mexico. They'd been killed in a house fire two years ago that Ana had barely escaped. She had no other family, and had avoided social workers by living on the street until she ended up at a shelter run by the local diocese.

I watched as she stood in the doorway, her eyes glued to Allie. She followed every move my daughter made, her mouth hanging open a little.

Mindy was leaning against the wall, breathing hard as she too watched Allie defend herself from the knives and swords that Marcus and Cutter were advancing with.

She blocked, parried, jumped, and kicked, deflecting every one of their advances. And with each thrust, my chest tightened painfully. I wished they would train with less lethal weapons—and I knew they did with the other students—but with Allie, it was no holds barred.

So far, she hadn't received a serious injury, which I considered a blessing, but it left open the question of whether or not her special genetics meant she would heal faster. Part of me hoped she would. Part of me didn't, because that just meant that she was even closer to her demonic lineage, something I hated thinking about, even if it did make her who she is today.

"Why is she even bothering to train?"

It took me a moment to realize that Ana was talking about Allie.

"Well, to get better, of course. To practice. To be ready."

"She looks pretty ready."

"She does, yeah. But fighting isn't just about the moves. It's also about the thinking. Her reflexes are good, but inside she's still mentally the same kid she was before."

"Before what?"

I turned to face her straight on. "I thought you knew."

Ana shrugged. "Not really. Not me, anyway. The others might. I heard about a battle. And something about going inside a catacomb and a gate to Hell that her blood closed. I'm not really sure how, but I guess maybe that's the kind of thing we're going to learn about here?"

"Absolutely that's the kind of thing."

"Yeah? Cool. That sounds pretty cool. Kind of like a video game."

"Kind of," I agreed. "Except really, really not."

That earned me a small smile. "Anyway, that's all I know."

"Well, that's about right. But the bigger truth is that before that day, she was just Allie. Or so we thought. There were all these gifts hidden inside her, and somehow when she went into those catacombs and used her blood to lock the gate, it made her better. Stronger and faster and all that good stuff. But to me she's still just Allie."

"So when did that happen?"

"Just a few months ago. Early summer."

"Wow. She got really good fast."

"She'd already been training. And the supernatural gifts helped, too."

"Yeah, I guess that would."

"Mindy's good, too. Have you been watching her?" I indicated the way she was sparring with Jared. "I'll tell you a secret. She kind of sucked when she started."

"Yeah? She looks good now."

"Yes, she does. And she's only been doing this for a few months, too. Seriously, anyway."

"Wow. That's cool."

"If she can do it, you can too," I told her. "You fought a hellhound and got away. That's major."

"Yeah?"

"Trust me. I've had more than one hellhound kick my ass."

She only shrugged, and I realized I'd lost her. *Trust me*, I'd said. But this girl wasn't ready to trust yet.

"They didn't believe you, did they?" I asked her.

"Who?"

"Whoever you told about the hellhound attack."

She made a rough noise in her throat. "No. Nobody believed me. At least not until that guy found me in the church shelter. I guess he heard about some crazy kid telling stories about a maniac dog creature."

"I'm glad he found you. And he did believe you. I believe you too. So does everyone here."

She didn't answer. But she didn't look away. And I might have imagined it, but I thought she smiled.

"Now, it's time for you to meet your teacher." I lifted my hand, and waved at Marcus, who was taking a break from sparring with Allie. As he signaled that he would be right over, Ana snorted. "I know him. He's the one who brought us here after that bitch Jessica killed Dani."

"Then, he was your escort. Now, he's your teacher."

"Hey, Ana," Marcus said as he approached us. "Ready to train?"

"Is that what this is? Training class time?"

Marcus and I exchanged a look. "For the first week, we're going to play this loose. Then we'll put together your actual schedules for the rest of the semester. Sound like a deal?"

She shrugged. "Whatever."

"So, is that a yes? I was thinking we'd do a quick run-through, and then I'll get you sparring with Mindy."

Her mouth hung open. "Today?"

I laughed. "You'll do great. I promise. Find me later and tell me about it, okay?"

"You really want to know?"

"Of course I do. That's what we're here for."

"Oh. Well, okay. That's cool."

She flashed me a tentative smile before following Marcus into the room. She had a long road. She didn't really trust us—who could blame her?—and she had terrible self-esteem. But she'd opened up, at least a little, and we'd had an actual conversation.

So maybe I wasn't going to totally suck at this job after all.

10

I spent the morning doing admin work until I thought my brain would explode. Then I checked on Timmy and Stuart, before snagging Allie and Eliza as co-escorts for our first patrol with the newbies.

"First question," I said before we piled into my ancient Odyssey van, "where should we go to look for a demon?"

Allie and Eliza both tightened their mouths, as if desperately trying not to blurt out the answer. The other three looked at each other, clearly bewildered.

"Um, Hell?" Ren suggested.

"Not a bad answer," I admitted. "The downside is that to get there we'd have to open a gate, and that's never good. Any other ideas?"

Once again the kids stared at each other as if I'd asked them to calculate pi to the twenty-seventh place.

"No worries. Let's go at this another way. Who knows how the demons become corporeal?"

That time, all three hands shot up. "Ana?"

"They live in the, um, ether. Like the air around us. And when someone dies, they go into the body."

"Good. Who wants to add to that?" I picked from the two hands that shot up again, calling on Bruce.

"But they can't enter the faithful. Those souls fight, and there's only a short window. So the demons usually get battled back.

"Yes. Exactly. Good on you guys."

"Marcus told us some stuff in the van. And I learned a little from the Hunter who recruited me," Ren said.

"Good. Then you're more prepared than a lot of recruits. Plus, at *Forza West,* you don't have to learn Italian. Always a perk."

The mansion was located on cliffs that overlooked the ocean, and I navigated the van down the winding street as I talked.

"So what does the process of how a demon becomes corporeal tell you about where we might find new demons?"

Once again the kids looked baffled.

"Come on, guys. You can do this."

"Um, they'll be where people are dead?"

I pointed at Ren, and then at my nose. "Absolutely. So where do people die?"

"Hospitals," they said in unison, then laughed. "And accidents," Ana added. "Like on the scene."

"And um, those places old people go. What do you call them?" Ren looked around at the group.

"Nursing homes," Bruce said.

"Good call," I said. "Nursing homes, assisted living facilities, hospices. Definitely demon magnets. But can anyone think of a way to scope specific locations? How can you increase your odds of finding one newly made? Easier to fight, still hasn't quite got the hang of his or her body."

"How?" Bruce asked. I caught of glimpse of him in the rearview mirror. He was leaning forward, looking fascinated.

"Hand out the papers, Eliza."

She bent over, then pulled out three copies of the local paper and passed one to the new students. "This is where Eric and I usually start. You want to tell them why?" I asked, looking at Allie.

She was sitting in the passenger seat beside me, and now she twisted around to talk. "Demons like to go back to where they were born. Born into a body, I mean. I don't know why, but they do, at least for the first couple of days. So if you can figure out where someone might have gotten infested with a demon, chances are you can go back and find them again."

"See what you find," I told the kids, who immediately started flipping through pages. It didn't take long. San Diablo is a relatively small town, and our paper is mostly filled with advertisements and schedules for various high school events. The actual news articles— especially about strange happenings—are easy to find.

Ren's hand shot up. "Check this out! Some tourists —a couple— reported a dead body by a dumpster in an alley off Main Street but by the time the cops got there, the guy was awake. Cops decided that the tourists were just wrong. Like the guy was dead drunk, but not actually dead. But the couple insisted they weren't. Apparently they volunteered at a hospice, and said they knew what a dead person looked like."

"Bingo," I said. "Mysterious deaths from which someone recovers. Horrible accidents that they walk away from. Surviving a drowning. All of those things tend to signal that there's a demon who's moved in. And if we get lucky, we just might meet him in that alley. Ready?"

Not only did the kids all say that they were, they all looked exceptionally eager. Again, I gave myself a pat on the back. So far so good.

The alley was off of Main Street, the anchor for the downtown touristy shopping area. I found a nearby parking space, then we all piled out and started heading toward the scene of the crime.

"If we find one, I'm going to take it. I want you guys to watch and learn. Next time, it'll be your turn." As I'd expected, each of them looked both relieved at not being on deck just yet, and excited about the possibility to come.

As soon as we entered the alley, I knew we were going to get lucky. A dark haired man was leaning against one of the commercial trashcans, his hands in his pockets. He was about thirty, and his build fit the description of the dead man. I gave the kids a stern look, and Allie held out an arm, signaling for them to stand back.

I took a step toward the probable demon. "Hey," I

said. "You may not know it, but there's a no loitering policy in San Diablo. We try to keep our streets and alleys safe. Lots of kids in this town."

He tilted his head as he looked me up and down. Then he stepped forward. He looked a little out of sorts, but there was no way I could be sure that he was a demon. Not yet.

He could be someone else entirely, and not the man from the newspaper report. Or, he could be that man, and simply passed out, just as the article said.

Get it wrong, and I could potentially kill a human, and that would be a pretty crappy first lesson for these kids. I wouldn't much like it, either.

Obviously I couldn't explain that to the kids, since narrating my thoughts would also give this possible demon knowledge of what I was up to. Fortunately, I'd had the foresight to fill a McDonald's to-go cup with holy water, and I held it up as I walked toward him, pretending I was nervous to be approaching a stranger.

"Listen, I just want to throw this trash away, and then we're going to get out of here. I don't know what your deal is, but you're kind of creeping me out hanging out by the dumpster."

Again he said nothing. I took one more step, feigned tripping, and managed to toss the contents of the cup all over the demon's face.

And he really was a demon. All doubts were erased as his face began to sizzle.

"Ha!" Allie's voice rang through the alley. "I knew it.

I totally knew it." Her words started a chain reaction of agreement from the other kids.

I ignored them. I had to, because the demon had taken a step toward me, his face contorted in pain, and right then, my only focus was on him. And on staying alive.

I shifted my weight, twisted, and got him in the gut with one swift kick. He flew backwards, his back slamming against the brick wall. I pulled the stiletto out of the little holster I'd sewn into the sleeve of my jacket. Then I aimed it for his eye.

"Kate, no!"

I stopped just a millisecond from releasing the knife. I took a step back, wary, but not willing to kill this creature until I knew how he knew me. By reputation? Or something else. "Who the hell are you?"

"You knew me as Thomas Duvall."

"Duvall?" That from Allie. She raced forward to stand beside me, then looked the demon up and down. "You're not Thomas Duvall."

"I am Quiric," he said, in that precise, steady cadence. "Duvall's body has long since gone. I had to speak to you."

"What's going on?" Bruce asked.

"We kind of met him. In Rome," Allie told him. "Before he got killed. He's a white hat demon. One of the good guys. At least for purposes of not wanting hell on earth." She turned back to Duvall-now-Quiric. "The gate's locked now. So how do we know we can trust you?"

"I have no proof to offer." His tone had turned reverential, and his eyes were on Allie. "But know this. I will never harm you. Not you or your mother. Or her mate, Eric."

"He's not my m—" I cut myself off. Really not the issue. "Why won't you harm us?" I asked instead.

"Because I closed the gate," Allie said, answering before Quiric could answer. "And Eliza? Would you harm her?"

Quiric's eyes narrowed. Eliza had tried to open the gate in a futile and misguided attempt to save her mother's life. "It is tempting," he said, looking at her. "But no. We understand her intention. And we know that she is one of yours."

"So are these," I said, indicating the students. "They are under my protection. You harm them, you will have no pass from me. You understand that?"

"I do not wish to find a new form. And our debt to you is great. Your companions are safe as well. At least from those who honor my name."

"Good. In that case, thank you for the detente."

"It is more than that," he said. "It is a bond. All you must do is say my name, Quiric, and those who stand with us will let you pass. This is not an offer we make lightly. You did what could not be done," he said to Allie. "And because of you, we continue to enjoy this realm, with its physical pleasures."

"We thank you," I said, stepping in for Allie. I took a moment, considering asking him to attack the students and show them what he could do, but I didn't want to risk one of the kids actually managing to take him out. Quiric and his compatriots would keep their word even if that happened, but it still seemed rude.

"We're going to be on our way," I told them. "Nothing against your kind, but I need to find a demon I can kill as a demonstration to these students."

I thought I saw him smile, but it may have just been a shadow. "Katherine, there is more. Those who stand with me do not wish to see this world turned into a hell dimension, as my brother demon, whom you knew as Tagelli, explained to you in Rome."

"I know," I told him. "And it was both our good fortune that our interests aligned."

"We also do not wish to be subjugated to the will of she who seeks to be corporeal. We are satisfied with our existence, but should Lilith manifest in this world, we will be required to be subservient to her."

"So she really is trying to become corporeal again," I said, a chill running through my body. I glanced over at the kids, all of whom were listening with rapt attention. I turned back to Quiric. "How? We destroyed the chalice stone. There's no other. Is she still trying to get into Allie? Is there a ceremony? What's her plan?"

"I cannot say if it is Allie she expects to be her vessel, but were I to guess, I would believe it so."

"And without the chalice stone, how is she going to do that?"

He shook his head. "I don't know. All I know is that she is preparing for the ritual. Putting the pieces in place."

"What pieces? I can't stop her if I don't have the information."

"Again, I do not know for certain. But there are rumors that she is seeking Solomon's Stone. That it would be sufficient to draw her essence from the ether for the merging."

Relief crashed over me. "Then we're safe. The stone shattered when Lilith first went after Eric as a body for her consort."

Thomas shook his head. "You would be wise, I think, not to assume that everything is as you believe, even if you have seen it with your own two eyes."

"Good advice. Thank you."

"I have no more to tell you, Katherine Crowe."

"It's Connor now."

His brow quirked and I saw a glint of the evil that was inside him, despite our civilized conversation. "Oh? Is it really?"

"Yes," I said, telling myself not to get angry. No matter what, this creature was a demon, and he knew how to play with thoughts and emotions.

"You should go now," I said. "Thank you for the warning, and the information."

He inclined his head. "Heed me. We will help you, but only so far as our interests align."

"I understand," I said, and then I watched in silence as he turned and walked away.

"Holy shit," Bruce said from behind me. "That was freaky."

"You're not wrong about that," I said as I turned to

115

the group. Allie was looking right at me, and I met her eyes. I saw her concern there as well. But also her excitement. We now knew that Lilith already had a plan to come back. In the abstract, that sucked. But it also meant that we were one step further along that we had been. Apparently there was a way, or at least Lilith thought there was. All we had to do now was identify the ritual, and figure out how to stop it.

Easy as pie.

"So, um, does this mean we're not killing demons today?" Ren looked at all of us, his expression unreadable. I wasn't sure if he was relieved or annoyed.

"It probably does. I need to get back and get the team researching this." I led them through the alley, planning to cut down the much less crowded side street to get back to where I'd parked the van. But just as we reached the end of the alley, something fast and lithe leaped toward me, grabbing me by the shoulders and slamming me back against the brick wall as another demon tumbled Allie to the ground.

I cried out in both pain and fear for my daughter, then rammed my leg up so that my knee caught the demon in the crotch. She jerked back, and I used her temporary distraction to grab her collar and spin us until she was the one against the wall. At the same time, I snapped my wrist, releasing the stiletto I'd returned to my sleeve, and raised it, the point just millimeters from her eye.

Beside me, I saw that Allie was in the exact same position and breathed a sigh of relief. In theory, I knew that

Allie was more than able to take care of herself. In practice, I would always worry.

"So, um, why aren't we killing them?" Allie asked.

"Class time," I said with a grin, then raised my voice so the kids could hear me. "So how do we know these are demons?"

In my peripheral vision, I watched them look at each other. They were standing behind Eliza, who'd clearly moved in to protect them when these two had come at Allie and me.

"Um, they attacked you," Bruce said.

"No, they could just be stupid muggers." That from Ana.

"Ana's right," I said. "And we don't kill humans. Not even criminals."

"Their breath is rancid," Allie said. "Smells like rotting fish. You guys come here take a whiff."

They all looked disgusted but did as told while Allie and I kept the demons still.

"The odor gets worse as the demon gets older. Who can say why?"

Ren's hand shot up.

"You can just answer," I told him.

"Because they're in a dead body. And so it's, like, decaying."

"Perfect answer," Allie said, and he stood up a little straighter.

Against the wall, my demon growled low in her throat. "Sorry," I said. "Class first. Then I'll get around to killing you."

"*Bitch.*"

"Hey, we don't talk that way in school."

As the demon glared at me, I glanced again at the kids. "Who has holy water?" As I'd hoped, all three of them did.

"Gold stars all around. Splatter them."

They started to fumble for their holy water, and I made a mental note to add a talk about how to carry your supplies.

"You can kill us, Hunter, but more of our kind will rise."

"Thank you," I said to the demon, then turned to the kids. "Forget the holy water. That was the best clue of all. Self-identification." The demon snarled. "So next question. How can I kill her?"

"Stab through the eye!"

"Beheading?"

"Fire?"

"All good answers. The first two would release the demon, leaving you with a human corpse. Fire would destroy the body, and the demon would most likely leave voluntarily. Excellent work."

I grinned at them. "You've passed the oral exam. Now let's see how you do on the practical." I nodded to Allie, and as if we'd planned it, we released the demons together and jumped back. "Time to get busy."

At first, my three students stood stock-still. Then one of the demons did an about face, and took off running past me toward the far end of the alley.

"Screw that," Ren said, tearing off after him. Ana

was right behind, going after the other one, who had taken the first's lead.

Bruce took a step forward, then stopped, as if he wasn't sure who to help. While he stood unsure, the other two nailed the assignment.

Ren knocked his demon completely flat on its back, all the while shouting "dammit, dammit, dammit," as he tried to free his school-assigned stiletto from his belt.

"Screw it," he said, then jabbed his finger through the beast's eye. He scooted backwards as the demon was expelled, muttering, "Gross! Gross! Gross!" even as he shot me an amazed—and proud—glance.

At the same time, Ana had been tossed against the brick wall by her demon. And though I expected Bruce to run in at that point to help her, she managed to push away, using the momentum to leap on the second demon like a toddler running for a parent.

Her legs wrapped around its waist so that they were face to face. She reached around and held its hair to steady herself, then used the stiletto that was already in her free hand to impale the beast. Immediately, the body went limp, and she fell to the ground, a huge grin on her face.

I watched, thrilled not only with their performance, but with the confidence those wins would give Ren and Ana. As for Bruce, I wasn't sure what held him back, and I walked over to check on him as Allie and Eliza helped the other two up, showering them with praise.

"You okay?"

"I feel like an idiot," he said, his voice hard. "I

couldn't decide who to help, so I didn't get into the game at all."

"Don't beat yourself up. Hesitation is normal, and this was all over pretty fast. You'll have plenty of time to get in there. I promise."

He looked me in the eye and nodded. "Yeah. Yeah, I know I will."

11

We returned from our odd hunting session to find Laura waiting for us. "You three are supposed to go train," she said to the newbies. "And the rest of you ... well, just go on into the dining room."

I expected her to come with us, but it was only me, Allie, and Eliza who went. I understood why when I pulled open one of the ornate double doors to see Father Donnelly seated at the huge table with Eric. That would have completely destroyed my day were it not for the elderly woman sitting with him.

"Signora Micari!"

She stood as Allie, Eliza, and I all rushed to greet her with enthusiastic hugs. The owner of a B&B near the Vatican, she had housed us on our recent trip. But more than that, she used to work as a housekeeper and pseudo-dorm mom when I was in *Forza*.

JULIE KENNER

Most recently, she'd been a key part in helping to locate and lock the gate to hell.

"Ah, you have grown," she said in her thick Italian accent as she looked Allie up and down. "In both body and skill, I understand."

Allie grinned, looking pleased as Signora Micari turned to me. "And, Kate. It is most good to see you again."

"You, too," I said honestly. "So don't take this the wrong way, but why are you here? The both of you," I added, with a hard glance toward Father Donnelly. He may have provided invaluable information in Rome, but that didn't mean I trusted him.

Signora Micari smiled. "Ah, Katherine, I am happy to say that Father Corletti suggested I come work for you. Now that I no longer have my bed and breakfast, he thought I would like to work with the students again."

I wanted to whoop with glee, but Allie already had done that, and she high-fived Eliza, who we'd originally met at that same B&B.

"Wait," I said. "What do you mean you don't have your bed and breakfast anymore?"

"Arson, I am afraid. As you might expect, there were some demons who were unhappy with the work we did."

"I am so sorry."

"As was I, but now it is all good. God provides, yes? And please. You and the students should call me Gabriela."

I looked at Eric, who shook his head with a smile. "I

don't think we can," he said. "You'll always be Signora Micari to us."

She laughed. "Very well."

"I just saw Quiric," I told her. "He has a new body now, obviously, but he wanted to let me know that the four of us can name drop if we're ever in a battle with a black hat demon."

"Well, that's some good news at least," Eric said. "Always good to limit the scope of our enemies."

"I'm sure he would've wanted me to give you his regards," I told Signora.

"It is good to know that he is corporeal once again. He might be a demon, but in many ways he was a good man. Certainly when our interests aligned," she added, and we all laughed.

"How about you?" Eliza asked Father Donnelly. "It's great to see you, but why are you here?" Unlike me, Eliza didn't have a problem with the priest. He had been her only help when she'd been trying to both rescue her mother and destroy the key that could open the gate.

"Yeah. Why are you here?" Allie's tone was less welcoming, considering what Father Donnelly had done to her father, and, ultimately, to her. I felt the same way. But he had been instrumental in Rome, providing us with historical information that had turned out to be crucial. So I was willing to cut him a little—very little—slack.

We all waited for him to answer, but it was Signora Micari who spoke as she stood. "I think it is best if I leave to go explore the kitchen. That is assuming you want me to stay?"

"Are you kidding? Of course we do." I glanced to Eric for confirmation, but he just held up his hands as if in surrender.

"You know I do, but it's your call, Kate. You're the headmistress."

I rolled my eyes, then turned back to the Signora. "Welcome to *Forza West*, Signora. I'm thrilled that you're here. Go check it out, tell us if there's anything you need, and thank you."

"I am so happy to be here," she said, aiming a bright smile at all of us before leaving the room.

"Okay," Allie said, once the signora left the room. She stared down Father Donnelly. "What's going on?"

She stood tall and strong, her hair pulled back into a tight ponytail and her mouth curved down in a scowl. My heart squeezed as I looked at her. She was taking charge, and I knew that as the years went by, she would be doing that more and more.

Father Donnelly nodded for us all to sit, and we did. But before he could start his explanation, there was something I needed to know. "How are we related?"

He sat back his eyes going wide. Clearly that was something he didn't realize I knew.

"How did you learn of this?"

"Wait, what?" Allie said, and I shot her an apologetic glance.

"I saw some of my mother's family's genealogical records when Eliza was moving up here. Not much. Just the name Donnelly, but under the circumstances it made sense."

He leaned back, his fingers steepled as he nodded.

"So it's true? You're related to a branch of the family that spins out to me, not just to Eliza?"

I had been holding onto the hope that Father Donnelly was related to Eliza on her paternal side, which would leave me without a hint of blood in common with the man. Apparently that wasn't the case.

"I am sorry if you find this news offensive," he said. "But, yes, we are family."

"No," I said. "We share blood. That doesn't make us family.

"I understand your animosity, Katherine I do. You feel that I overstepped bounds when I worked with Eric's parents on our—"

"Breeding program?" I put in.

I had taken a seat beside Eric, across from Father Donnelley, and now he took my hand under the table and squeezed.

"I don't disagree with you, Katherine."

"Call me Kate. Only Father Corletti calls me Katherine."

"But I did have my reasons." He paused, clearly debating. When he spoke again, there was resignation in his voice, and I knew that, finally, I'd hear the whole story. "The gate that Allie locked. It was conjured."

I looked at Eric but he only shook his head. I turned and looked the other direction at Eliza. Maybe this was something she'd heard about from her mother or her aunt, my mother. But she shook her head, too.

"Yes, conjured," Father Donnelly said. "My great grandparents many times removed along with Eric's. They were all four Demon Hunters with *Forza*. They were working to try and find an alchemical or magical way to bind demons. Instead, they accidentally created portals into various hell dimensions."

I leaned back in my chair, aghast. Beside me Allie and Eliza both made small gulping noises. "You mean they *opened* a gate," Eliza said. "One that already existed."

"No. They did not open one of the gates mentioned in either mythology or the Old Testament. Those are closed, to be opened only with keys that as far as we know do not exist in our world and must be conjured. While a risk, those gates are relatively safe. Their doors have never been flung wide open."

"They created a new gate," I said. "Oh, God."

"Indeed. They created five, and though our ancestors did manage to close these gates, some demons were able to cross over."

"How did they lock them?" Eric asked.

"They conjured mystical keys. But unlike the truly ancient gate keys, these keys still exist hidden in this world. No one knows where. Even our ancestors didn't know to where the keys disappeared once the ritual to close the gates was completed."

"Then how did they know they still existed?" Allie asked.

"I do not know. I know only that they were certain."

"And they were right. My grandmother found one," Eliza said. "Remember? And she hid it in the altar so the demons couldn't get it and open the gate."

"Exactly. Even with the keys hidden, our ancestors feared that these gates would be opened again in the future. And the conjured gates were much more invasive into our world than the gates into hell that had already existed for millennia."

"What do you mean?" Eric asked.

"Imagine Jupiter. The rings around it. When a natural gate into the hell dimension is accessed, it goes first to Jupiter's rings. The conjured gates gate skipped those rings altogether and went straight to the surface of Jupiter."

"It's not the greatest analogy, Father," I said, "but I get it. You're saying that instead of opening onto your basic hell dimension like the ether all around us, this gate opened to what we've been calling Uber-hell. The hell dimension where a demon like Lilith would exist in her true form. A dimension from which it usually takes centuries—or more—for a demon to leave."

"Exactly."

"Well, that completely sucks," Allie said, which I thought nicely summed up the situation.

"I'm sure they thought so as well," Father Donnelly said. "And according to what has been handed down in the family, they worked and studied and experimented to no avail trying to find a way to not only lock the gate should the keys manifest, but to create a breed of hunter capable of fighting what might come through."

Allie raised her hand. "Me. They were trying for me."

He nodded. "They knew that any demon coming from that realm would be stronger, more dangerous and more inclined to destroy humanity rather than mingle within it in the form of a human."

"And it took generations for them to figure it out." That from Eliza who was leaning forward intently.

"Yes. A method by which they were confident they could imbue additional strength into a hunter. A strength that would be genetically transferred to that endowed hunter's progeny." He nodded from Eric to Allie. "And that progeny, while having strength, would also have the blood that could act as a permanent lock for the conjured gates."

"So what I did in Rome—that only locked that one gate for good? The others can still be opened?"

"Only if the key is found."

"One key was found," Eric reminded him. "The others could be, too."

"Indeed. And *Forza* has been seeking to find their mystical hiding place for centuries to no avail. Which is both good and bad. Find them, and we can destroy them, thereby ensuring the gates stay closed. But finding them brings them into this world."

"And then there's the danger that the bad guys would get it. And then the only hope would be Allie's blood."

"Indeed." He met her eyes. "You will, of course, be expected to have children."

Her eyes went wide. "Um, hello. Sixteen," she said at

the same time that Eric shoved his chair away and stood. "And just barely. So, yeah. Not breeding."

"We are not having that conversation. My daughter is not your breeding stock."

"You know that it is a discussion that must be had. But you are right. We do not have to talk about it now."

"Mom?"

"It's okay, baby," I said, trying to control my own temper. I turned to Father Donnelly. "Right now, our focus is on protecting Allie. Lilith wants to bind with her again. That happens, and your secret weapon becomes useless. And guess what?" I added, as my anger rose. "The reason Lilith *can* get into my daughter is because of what you did. So, yes, you bred a child capable of fixing the screw-up of our ancestors. She saved the world. But she saved it at one hell of a price."

To his credit, Father Donnelly looked genuinely contrite. "I know. And I am sorry about what was done to you. But my family—and yours, Kate, Allie, Eliza— our ancestors created this problem along with Eric's."

"But my parents were trying to stop you," I told him. "They were in Rome to keep you from performing the ritual on Eric."

"They were, yes. They agreed that we needed a way to lock the gate permanently. To render the missing keys ineffective. But they didn't agree with our method."

"Gee, maybe that's because your method involved putting a demon in a child," I snapped.

"And that child grew up to be Allie's father," he retorted, his voice hard and sharp. "And if we hadn't—if

Eric were not what he is now—then this world would be in ruin now. Because Allie wouldn't exist in the way she does now. She might not exist at all. She would not have been here to close the gate."

"You think that makes it right?"

"No. I think it makes us lucky."

"You put a demon inside me." Eric's voice was tight.

"I do regret the pain it has caused you. It should not have. Had you not encountered the Cardinal Fire, the demon inside you would have stayed bound. You would not have suffered the way that you have. For that I am truly sorry."

"You only think that's the case. It might have burst free at any time. You ran one hell of a risk."

To his credit, Father Donnelly nodded. "It is in the past now. I can change nothing. I can only give you my apologies for the pain. As for the fact that Allie now exists—that she is a remarkable young woman with incredible skills—for that I will not apologize."

"You can't control me," Allie said.

"No, you are right. And we are blood, child, and I wish only good things for you. If you choose not to follow this path I would not fault you," he said, though I didn't believe him. Not after his comment about Allie's children.

"But I hope you stay on this path," he said. "There is a storm of demons coming. More High Demons are breaking through to this world. You have seen this. You've fought this. We assume that some are coming through cracks in remaining gates."

I met Eric's eyes. *Not good. Really not good.*

"My hope is that we can find those gates—and their keys—and seal them. That *you* can seal them."

"I hope that means you're going to help fight Lilith," I said. "Allie can't do any of that if a High Demon's inside her."

He nodded. "Of course I will help. I'm in San Diablo now, after all."

"Yeah, why is that?"

"Honestly? I wanted to be closer to you. I wanted to be part of your fight. To make amends, perhaps. And because you will need my help, I think."

Eric frowned. "In general, or..."

"San Diablo seems to be one of the focal points for increased demonic activity. It seemed practical to be here."

I leaned forward. "You think that means a gate is here? Leaking hell-goo?"

"It's possible. Or it could be something else." He drew a breath "For generations, our families have fought demons. They excelled at it. Were renowned for it. Allie will outshine them all. Don't walk away, child. You are here for a purpose."

"All I wanted was to do was what my mom did. I never wanted to be this super fighter. What if I want a different path? A different purpose."

"Do you?"

She looked at me and her father, then shrugged. "I don't know. I wanted in, I did. I practically begged."

"I remember," I told her gently.

"But I thought I'd be one of many. Like serving in an army."

"You're still part of a team, baby," Eric said. "Look where you are. Think about who has your back."

She looked across the table at Father Donnelly. "I don't like what you did. But I understand why you did it. Why our ancestors did. But I haven't forgiven you. I might never forgive you." She pushed away from the table. "I'm going to go find Mindy. To Eliza she said, "Want to come with?"

Eliza nodded, and they stood. I watched them before turning back to Father Donnelly.

"And you, Kate? Eric? Do you understand? Will you forgive?"

I started to say never, but Eric spoke first. "You're right about one thing. What you did—what our families did—that led to Allie and who she is. And for her sake," he said, his voice grave, "I'll forgive most anything."

12

hile Eric took all of the kids on a tour of the library, I went to see Stuart.

Nancy looked up as I stepped in, then smiled brightly at me. "Timmy is playing over there," she said, nodding toward the attached bedroom. "He's being an absolute sweetheart."

I glanced around the partially open door. Sure enough, Timmy had spread all of his cars and stuffed animals over the floor and arranged them into, as far as I could tell, some sort of imaginary town.

He waved happily when he saw me, then went back to whatever important work he was doing.

"Thank you so much for watching him today," I said, turning my attention back to Nancy. "I know that's not what you signed on for. I need to focus on finding someone to act as a nanny during the workday. As you can probably tell, we launched this school a little bit earlier than we'd intended. Things are still crazy."

"Oh, it doesn't bother me at all, dear. He's quite the little angel." She nodded towards Stuart. "Nothing, I'm afraid. I was hoping he'd speak to me as he did to you, but sadly no. Has he said anything else to you?"

I hadn't told Nancy about Stuart, and it felt a little odd that she knew. It seemed like a secret, but that was ridiculous. She was his nurse now, and she needed complete information. As for how, I assumed Eddie told her, or Rita had. Through Eddie, of course.

She stood. "Why don't I take a little break so you can spend some time? I'll go get a cup of coffee downstairs. I believe Rita's with Eddie, I'll go find them for a chat."

"I appreciate that," I told her. "And you're lucky. Our new cook just arrived. Senora Micari. You should find her in the kitchen as well."

"That sounds lovely." She turned to face my husband. "Stuart, Kate is here. Don't you want to wake up for her?"

I smiled at her words, feeling both grateful that she was here and melancholy. With every day that passed, I was coming to terms with the probability that I wouldn't get Stuart back. Even despite his inexplicable talking, hope kept moving farther and farther away.

As she left the room, I popped my head again into the connecting bedroom. "You good, kiddo?"

"A-okay, Mommy!"

"I'm going to talk to Daddy for a while, you come in here if you need anything, okay?"

He saluted, with an, "Aye aye, Captain!"

I turned away grinning, and was still smiling as I pulled a chair up next to Stuart's bed.

"I really wish you were awake," I told him. "I just had a long talk with Father Donnelly. Yeah, he's here, and he's still not on my favorite person list. I know that shocks you. But I guess I can understand why he did what he did. Sort of."

I thought about that, then amended, "*Understand*, yeah. But I'm still not sure I can forgive it."

I took his hand wondering if he was going to respond to anything I said, but he didn't. His fingers just hung limp inside mine. I tried not to let myself be disappointed.

"The new kids seem good. A little green, but surprisingly eager, and they did well in their first battle. Granted, Allie and I were there watching the whole time, but they did good. Bruce seemed a little hesitant, which surprised me but—"

I cut myself off. Stuart didn't even know who these kids were, and I felt like an idiot saying all of this to him.

At the same time I wanted him to know what was going on. I wanted to believe that he was listening and would come out of this with full knowledge of everything that had transpired while he'd been sleeping. So I drew a breath and forced myself to go on, despite the lump in my throat.

"I like all of them, but I've gotten to know Ana the best so far, which isn't saying much. It's been barely five minutes, but she seems like a good kid. She's quiet, and she needs more confidence. But she's got solid skills to build on. I think she might be interested in *alimentatore* training, but I suppose it's too early to know.

"I haven't spent as much time with Ren, but from what Marcus and Jared tell me, he's got great potential. He wants to please everyone though, which is great for us as teachers, but bad for him. I need to figure out a way to give him that loner know-it-all vibe. That's important for a Hunter. Trusting yourself."

I thought about my words, then squeezed his hand again. "I guess you learned that one the hard way, huh? I mean where hunting is concerned, Demon Hunters have to trust themselves most of all. I'm sorry if that bled into our marriage. That loner thing. The secrets. I know you get it. Now, at least. But back then, I kept so much from you, and I'm sorry. I hope you really understand, and forgive me. I only kept the secrets because it was all on me, and—*oh!*"

He was squeezing my hand.

"Stuart!"

His grip seemed to tighten, and as I looked at his face his lips moved.

I bent forward, trying to hear. His whole body seemed to shake with the effort of wanting to get words out.

"Stuart," I said leaning forward. "You can do it. Wake up. Talk to me. You can do it."

"Cat." His voice was raspy. *Did he just say cat?*

"D-d-d-dog."

I gaped at him. This was really making no sense.

His head lurched up and he burst out, "RAT," so loud it was practically a scream. Then he fell backward, his body going limp again as he released my hand.

"*Daddy! Daddy, Daddy!*" Timmy ran into the room, Boo Bear flying at his side. "Did Daddy talk?"

I realized I was already standing. I scooped him up and held him close, my arms wrapped tight around him. "He talked a little, baby. But then he stopped again." I pulled him back just enough so that I could see his sweet face, and my heart broke at the tears in his eyes.

"Will Daddy get better?"

I wanted to lie but I couldn't. "That's what we're praying for."

"I pray too. Should I kiss and make it better?"

"It can't hurt, kiddo." I was having a hard time keeping my voice steady.

I lifted him up and put him on the bed beside Stuart. He bent over and very gently gave Stuart a butterfly kiss on each cheek and then a kiss on his nose. I blinked rapidly, forcing myself not to cry. I didn't want him to see me like that.

But then he turned to me, and I couldn't help it, and hot tears began to stream down my cheeks.

"Want me to kiss and make Mommy better too?"

My nose started to run. "Yes, please," I managed to say.

He held up his arms and I scooped him off the bed, desperately needing his kisses. Then I hugged him close and almost—almost—forgot about the pain and the loss and the fear.

Gently, I pulled him away, then kissed his forehead before settling him on the ground. "Mommy has to go to work," I said. "Let's go find Ms. Nancy."

I took Timmy's hand once more, then turned to leave, only to find Nancy in the doorway, holding a thermal cup of coffee. She set it down on a small table by her chair that already had a book of crossword puzzles, a pencil, and a romance novel.

"All done?"

"Yeah. I need to get to work. You'll let me know if anything changes?"

"Of course, I will. Are you taking Timmy, or is he going back to his city?"

I grinned. Apparently I'd been right about the town. "I'll leave him with you, if you're sure it's no trouble."

"Of course it's no trouble. He's just playing in the room next door while I sit here and read or do my puzzles. It's nice to have the company."

"Thank you," I said sincerely, then stepped out of the room and headed down the hall. I'd reached the staircase landing when I saw Rita and Eddie coming up.

"Your cousin is a godsend," I told Rita. "A huge asset here at the, um, school," I don't know why I stumbled. Probably afraid I would have tossed *demon hunting* in there, and I had to keep reminding myself that Rita didn't actually know what we were doing here.

"I'm just trying to help the folks who matter to my Eddie."

I glanced at her Eddie, and he blushed, then scowled at me. I fought a grin, knowing I was never going to let him live that blush down.

"I'm going to pop in and tell her goodbye," Rita said. "I'm about to head out."

While she headed into the room, I stayed behind with Eddie. "*My* Eddie?" I said, emphasizing the possessive pronoun. "Is there something you want to tell me? Do I hear the tinkle of wedding bells?" I continued as his glower deepened. A glower that, I noticed, was softened by the light in his eyes. "Wait a second ... did you two drive here together?"

"Watch it, girlie," he said, "Or I'll have you planning the big day."

I took a step back, both surprised and not surprised at the same time. Mostly, I was delighted. "Eddie! Really?"

He made a shushing sound and I pulled him to the side. "Have you asked her?"

"Nope. But, she's the one. Took long enough to find her."

"Well, you've had a busy life. I guess you were just looking in all the wrong places."

"Guess it was a good thing you dragged me out of that damned Coastal Mists."

"I guess it was," I said, and we shared a smile. After a moment I tilted my head and shifted my expression to one more serious. "You have to tell her before you ask," I said.

"Yeah, well, too late for that. It's a done deal."

"What? You said you hadn't asked."

"Didn't." He grinned, his bushy eyebrows waggling. "My Rita's a modern woman. She popped the question to me when I told her I was staying behind with Eric in the house."

"And you said yes without telling her everything?"

He shrugged. "Eh, just figured I needed to find the right time. Don't worry. I'll tell her. And when I do—when we get married and she moves into your house with me—well, I'll want Eric to move out. We'll need our alone time. Plus he should be here."

"Eddie...."

He shook his head, "I mean it. This little romance novel intrigue you have going on between you and your husband and your other husband—well, you need to put that aside. Other than Allie, he's the best fighter you've got. And yeah I'm including you. You're good but he's bigger and stronger. Even with that cane and that bad eye, that man has skills."

"I agree, but I don't know if it's the best idea for Eric to move in here."

He snorted. "You're thinking with parts south of your heart, girlie. You need to do what's best for this school and protecting these students. There's more kids coming, remember. You need a big enough team on-site to keep them safe. All that emotional hoo-ha? That's just your cross to bear."

I wanted to argue. I wanted to tell him that all of my southern parts were staying out of this conversation. But that would be a lie.

Besides, I didn't get the chance to tell him. Because just as I was trying to gather all of my confusing and overly emotional thoughts, the school siren started to blare, and the emergency light above Stuart's room started flashing.

13

I raced into Stuart's room to see his body lurching in the bed as he tried desperately to get air despite the way Nancy was holding her hand over his nose and mouth.

"What are you doing!?" I shouted as I sprinted in that direction.

Rita was faster though. I hadn't seen her from my angle, but she'd been by the emergency panel, and right as I reached the middle of the room, she grabbed her cousin around the waist and pulled her back.

Nancy turned, snarling, but Rita didn't flinch. Instead, she took the pencil I'd seen by Nancy's cross-word book, and shoved it straight into her cousin's eye.

I stood gawking, my mouth hanging open as the demonic shimmer filled the air and Nancy's body collapsed to the floor.

Rita took a step back, shaking her head and making a

cluck-clucking noise as she looked up at me, her expression both sad and energized. "Poor Nancy," she said.

"How—?" I began, but was cut off by Eric and Cutter, who barreled into the room, followed by the kids they'd been training.

"What's going on?" Eric asked. "Kate? Rita?"

"My Rita got the bitch," Eddie said. "The demon. Not Nancy. Good woman. May she rest in peace."

Eric looked at me, and I nodded.

Rita took a deep breath, smoothed her gray curls into place, and moved to Eddie's side. He put his arm around her. "You okay, sweetie?"

"I'm fine dear," she says, patting his arm. She looked up at me and shook her head. "I am so sorry. I noticed her complaining of indigestion when she came down for coffee, but I didn't think anything of it. Now I think it must have been a heart attack. Poor thing, she went into the restroom. When she came back out, I thought she seemed a little off. I guess one of those beasties ended up inside her. It does seem to happen a lot in this town."

I gaped a bit more. "You know about that?" I turned to Eddie. "Did you tell her? I thought you didn't tell her."

Rita waved away my words. "Eddie didn't say a thing. But I've seen a lot of strange things in my time, sugar. After I saw this kind of thing once or twice, I did a little poking around. I watched you, in fact," she said. "And my Eddie."

I frowned at Eddie even as I made a mental note to

try to be stealthier. Probably not going to happen, but at least I was noting it.

She looked at Eddie. "Demons, right?"

Eddie looked at me. "Told you. She's a helluva woman."

"So, I guess congratulations are in order?" I asked. After all, the woman knew his dark secrets.

"Congratulations?" Eric repeated. "For killing the demon? Good job by the way."

I shot him a quick glance, and he shrugged, clearly as out of sorts by this revelation of Rita's hidden skills as I was.

"We're getting hitched," Eddie said. "But don't any of you dare make a fuss about it."

"Of course we will," I said. "But later."

He snorted as I looked over at the bed, hoping all this activity had pulled Stuart out of his comatose state, but apparently it hadn't. He was breathing fine now, his chest rising and falling. But no sign that he was awake or inclined to talk.

So why was Nancy so intent on killing him?

It was a question I wanted to raise to Eric, but then I realized the answer: Stuart.

I was about to share that insight with Eric, but all of the students were gathered by the door, fascinated by this turn of events.

Instead, I went the practical route. "Rita, what do you want to do with the body? If we call the police and say that she had a heart attack, they're going to ask about the pencil in her eye."

"Oh. Goodness. I never thought about that." She looked at Eddie. "What do you usually do about that?"

"We have ways," he said. "I'll tell you about them later." He looked to Eric. "Can you take care of it? And maybe get an urn, so that Rita can spread her cousin's remains. Nancy was a good woman. She didn't deserve to have one of those beasties in her."

"I can," Eric said. "I will."

"Can they get into anybody?" Rita asked.

Eddie screwed up his mouth, like he didn't want to tell her the hard truth. "Theoretically, yeah, if they try hard enough. But there's only a short window after death for them to come in. The faithful, their souls tend to fight hard to protect their bodies long enough for the window to close. But those without faith..."

Rita nodded slowly. "Well, that's it then. Nancy was a lovely woman, but she didn't believe in anything. My goodness, she didn't even really believe in herself. Sweet and helpful, but she never really saw beyond the moment, you know?"

"Yeah," Eddie said, reaching over to squeeze her hand, his expression more tender than I'd ever seen on him. "I know."

Rita's smile lit the room, and I glanced at Eric, only to find that same expression on his face. And he was looking right at me.

As Cutter led the kids back to the training room—all talking among themselves about The Incredibly Exciting Drama they'd just witnessed—I tugged Eric to the side. "I was here in Stuart's room right before this happened," I said. "He squeezed my hand again. He talked again."

"You're sure?"

"Of course I'm sure," I snapped.

"Sorry. I know you are. What did he say?"

"It was nonsense. At least I think it was. But he seemed earnest. Like he was trying to find the right word."

"Kate. What did he say?"

"He said *cat,* and then he said *dog,* and then he said *rat*, like he'd just found the right word. Like he had to force it out. He's in there, Eric, but he can't get out. And he's trying to tell me something."

"You may be right."

"But why on earth would he be desperate to tell me about a rat?"

"I have no idea. Rats can be symbolic, and not always for the bad. Wisdom, tenacity, survival."

"Maybe that's it. He wants us to know he survived. That he's in there."

"Maybe." He sounded dubious.

"Well, if not that, then what?"

"Honestly, Kate, I don't know. How can I know?"

I threw up my hands. "Because that's your job," I said, the pitch of my voice rising even as more tears filled my eyes. "To know things."

"Katie, oh, Katie." He pulled me to him, then held me close, his hand lightly stroking my back.

"I'm sorry," I murmured, relishing his comfort even though I knew I shouldn't be. In these last months, I'd been relying on Eric's strength. And, I feared, I'd let him get closer than he should. No, not *let*. I'd wanted him. Needed him. And we'd fallen back into familiar patterns even though I knew I shouldn't. I was married. My husband was alive. Maybe even more alive than we'd believed. And yet I'd wanted it. Eric's familiar comfort and his unwavering strength.

No.

I pulled myself free, then glanced down at the floor. "Sorry. Everything's just coming at me from all sides, and I don't have answers about anything."

"I know. Tell me more."

I drew a breath and forced myself to focus. "He seemed to struggle to get the word out. And now Nancy tried to kill him. So I'm thinking the demons want to keep him silent. That somehow, they're strangling his voice. Or trying to."

"That makes sense. Come on. Let's hit the library. See what we can find about channeled speaking. Maybe he's in an altered state, maybe he's channeling demons. Hell, maybe he's channeling angels or having visions. I don't know."

He lifted two fingers to his forehead and started to rub. I reached for his other hand and squeezed. "I'm so sorry."

"Good God, Katie, you don't have anything to be sorry for. I wish I had answers for you. Whatever this is, I think it's important. Come on."

He led me out of the room and down the hall. I hurried to keep up with his long stride.

"Important how?" I asked.

"Not sure. At first I thought it was nothing. A medical anomaly, maybe. I even thought that it was you. Exhaustion and wishful thinking."

"You know me better—"

"I do. I'm sorry. But my point is, now it seems like it means something. Like Allie does need to be careful. She needs to focus on staying safe. And as for rat ... well that one I just don't know."

"Same thing, maybe? That Allie needs to survive? From what Father Donnelly said, that's pretty true. She's important. More important than we knew."

"Or it could be a traitor."

We were halfway down the stairs when he said that, and I stopped to look at him. "What do you mean?"

"There are a lot of new people in our lives now, Kate. We don't know anything about them. Not really. Hell, the furniture assemblers attacked us."

I hugged myself. He wasn't wrong.

"Maybe we haven't been careful enough. Maybe we've been relying on the fact that we have skills. But think about what we're up against. If there's a traitor in our midst, we could have a big problem."

"But who?" The minute I asked the question, I knew it was foolish. We had a team of six who handled maintenance and IT stuff, though only one came in daily during working hours to make sure the computer and security system worked. The others worked at the cathedral but were on call. And all had been vetted by the Vatican.

As for the housekeeping, that was the same deal. A staff of four, all of whom worked during school hours and lived on site in the guest cabana behind the building. All had begun their careers with *Forza* in Rome. They'd wanted to move to different locations, but they hadn't been fired, they hadn't left.

Soon, we'd have medical staff, too, but only one doctor would live on site. And they weren't even here yet. Same with Signora Micari who would have two helpers in the kitchen eventually.

As far as I was concerned, the odds of a traitor within the staff seemed pretty slim.

I said all that to Eric, thinking out loud, my voice low.

"I know," he said. "But can we really be too careful?"

"I suppose not."

"Come on. Let's get to the library. I want to get on the computer and talk where no one can overhear us."

But just as he said the words, Mindy and Laura walked by. They looked up at us. "Are you coming to the library? We were going to go do some research on San Diablo. See if maybe we can find out if there is a gate."

I'd filled Laura in on everything Father Donnelly had said, but I hadn't expected her to jump into research-mode so quickly. And as much as I loved and trusted my bestie, I didn't want anyone knowing about Stuart's strange rat proclamation. Not yet.

"No," Eric said, apparently reading my mind. "We were just going to get some coffee. We have some paperwork to go over."

"Ugh," Laura said. "Have fun."

As soon as they passed by, I turned to Eric. "I don't think it's them," he said. "But they don't need to know yet."

Once again, I was reminded of how well we'd meshed as a team. "Agreed," I said. "Do you really want coffee?"

"No. Come on." He led me back up the stairs to my bedroom. Timmy was with Eddie and Rita, so Timmy's attached room was just as empty as mine. "You have a school laptop, right?"

"Um," I said, but he'd found it by the time I remembered where I'd tossed the thing. Not great friends, technology and me.

He carried it to the sofa, then opened it on his lap. I sat beside him, watching. He turned to smile at me as we waited for the machine to log on as him. "I hate the circumstances," he said. "But this is kind of like old times."

I didn't answer. His statement felt too right to acknowledge. Instead, I nodded at the laptop. "So what are we databasing?"

He chuckled. "We really need to teach you how to talk tech."

"You know what I mean," I asked as the *Forza West*

screen popped up and he navigated to his personal area. "What are you looking for?"

"Honestly, I'm not sure. I'm logged into *Forza's* main search engine. Let me do a search for incidents involving sleep talking or speech from a comatose patient."

He typed a bit, then looked up at me. "I've already done this, you know. I'm doing it again just in case I missed something. Changing up a few parameters. But I don't expect we'll find anything. Still, it's a good place to start."

"You already tried this? Why didn't you tell me?"

"Of course I did. It's Stuart, and you love him, and there's something going on with him."

"You believed me. Even that first day, you believed me."

"I've always believed you, Katie."

"I know. Thank you. This is all very strange."

He reaches over and presses his hand against my back. I scoot closer, telling myself I just want to see the screen better.

"Yes," he said, his voice soft. "Very strange."

For the next few minutes, he typed and I tried not to be impatient. We came up with absolutely nothing, and he sighed, then told me he was going to change a few more parameters. "If he's warning about the future, maybe he's channeling an oracle."

He typed, then hit enter, then turned to me with a grin as a half-dozen hits filled the screen.

"Okay, now we might be getting to something." He

tapped the screen. "Check out this one. A dead man spoke."

I shifted, taking my eyes off the computer. The way he was bouncing around in the text was making me queasy. "Stuart isn't dead."

"True, but this account is from the fifteenth century. The *Forza* investigators are calling him dead, but there's some suggestions in the text that he was in a coma. They might not have understood the difference back then, and the patient's breathing may have been extremely shallow."

"What else does it say?"

He reaches out and tugs a lock of my hair. "I changed my mind. This isn't at all like old times."

"Excuse me?"

"You never gave a flip about what was in the books before."

I laughed, and he took my hand, his thumb lightly brushing my skin in a way that felt decidedly intimate.

For a moment, I let him touch me that way. For a longer moment, I want him to touch me more. Then I remembered myself and pulled my hand away, conjuring what I hoped was a casual-looking smile.

"So what happened?"

He cleared his throat. "Well, our *Forza* investigator didn't actually witness it, but he reports that several of the town's residents said that they would come to see the dead man to hear what he had to say. And each time, he spoke the truth."

"Oh. Wow."

"But...." He trailed off as he read some more.

"Well?" I was nothing if not impatient. "What did he tell them?"

"According to this, the words he spoke were true, but it also sounds like the statements were a lot like a fake psychic. The things they say can be interpreted in different ways depending on the circumstances and what the hearer wanted to be said."

I leaned back. "So no help to us. It's not as if we can know for sure."

"It's something, though. Maybe Stuart really is acting like a relay, sending warnings or messages."

"I don't know if that makes me feel better or worse. Especially since we don't know who the messages are from. Is it Lilith sending them? God? Maybe just Stuart inside his head trying to figure things out?"

I ran my fingers through my hair. "It could be something we don't even understand yet. Or maybe it's nothing at all, just his brain fumbling around trying to find his way back to consciousness."

I bit my lower lip, warding off tears as Eric looked at me, his expression hard but his gaze soft. "What?"

"I was wrong. This is like old times, after all."

"What are you talking about?"

"Me reading and doing the research, and you taking everything in, spinning it around, and coming out with something brilliant."

"I hardly think I'm being brilliant. More like confused and frustrated."

"Fair enough. But what you were saying, it helps. It

gets me thinking. And what I'm thinking is that you may be right."

I shook my head. "Right how?"

"We don't know why Stuart is talking, but I think there is a reason. It's not random."

"Then what is it?"

He shrugged.

"That's it? That's all you know?"

He shook his head, then closed the laptop and set it aside. "No. That's not all."

"Then what?"

"I know that I miss you. I'm sorry," he continued, his hand on my thigh as he moved closer. "I know you don't want me to say it, but it's true."

"Eric..." His name was meant to be a protest, but I didn't move away. "You miss me, too," he said.

"You know I do. But—"

He pressed his finger to my lips. "I'm going to kiss you, Katie. Stop me now if you really want to, but honestly, I don't think you do."

He was right. Damn me, he was right. And though I knew I would hate myself forever, I leaned in and lost myself in the pleasure of Eric's kiss. Of being in the arms of the first man I'd ever loved. A man who, I knew, could erase all my fears and doubts, even if only for a little bit.

He deepened the kiss, pulling me closer, his hands roaming my body until I could no longer think about right or wrong, grief or love. Until all I knew was Eric, his touch so familiar even in this new body.

I want to say there was guilt. I want to be the woman

who at least hesitated. But I didn't. He was my husband returned to me. One of two men I loved desperately. And when he carried me to the bed, I knew Eric was the only thing I wanted in that moment. Our love had survived death, and being together was a sacrament.

"I love you, Kate," he said later as we held each other naked under the covers. "Please tell me you don't regret that."

"Would you understand if I did?"

"Of course," he said, stroking my cheek as we looked at each other.

"Thank you." I swallowed, hating what I had to admit. "And I don't regret it." I leaned forward and kissed him. "Well, maybe a little. It's all very confusing."

"I know. When hasn't our life been confusing or challenging?"

"When we moved to San Diablo," I told him. "The years before you died."

"Oh, those were challenging," he said. "You're just blocking the potty-training phase and the screaming phase and the *Barney* phase. *That* was more challenging than the most aggressive demon."

I laughed. "You have a point."

We shared a smile, both of us thinking about the past. But my smile faded as I returned to the present. "I don't regret this," I told him. "But it can't happen again."

His mouth quirked up at the corner as he rolled on top of me. "Not even one last time?"

I squealed with laughter, then hooked my arms

around his neck. "Not even," I said. "But maybe one last kiss."

"I can live with that," he said, then leaned forward, his lips brushing mine. I arched up, wanting more despite my stern words.

"Eric," I murmured, sliding my arms down his back. "I think maybe—"

"Mom! Mom! He's awake! Stuart's—Oh!"

The moment the door burst open Eric had rolled off of me. But there was no hiding the fact that we were in bed. And not dressed.

Allie stood staring at us, and in that moment, she looked more like an adult than I had ever seen. "Allie," Eric began, but she held up a hand.

"No. Not right now. I don't know whether to be happy or freaked out. So not right now, okay?"

Eric nodded as I said, "He's really awake?"

"Yes. Just now. You have to come."

"Go get Eddie. We're right behind you."

She nodded. "Okay. Bruce and Ren were with me when I went in. Bruce is with him now, but I think Ren ran out to get you," she said with a hard look to her father.

"Go," Eric said. "The sooner you go, the sooner we can get there."

Her cheeks turned slightly pink, obviously realizing we needed to dress, and she zipped out of the room.

"Oh God," I said throwing the covers aside and practically leaping into my clothes as guilt and confusion and more guilt washed over me. "I can't believe we—"

"*No*," he said. "Not now. No guilt, no waffling. Not now. This needs to be about Stuart."

He was right. I shoved my feet into my shoes, then sprinted out of the room, Eric following as we practically flew the short distance to Stuart's room.

I paused to draw a breath and calm myself, then I stepped inside the mostly empty room, with only Stuart in his bed, sitting up and looking bewildered.

Wild relief crashed over me as I saw that he was really awake. I ran to him, taking his hands. "Oh my God, Stuart," I said, pulling him to me and hugging him.

"*Oh*," he said, and I heard the pain in his voice.

I backed away, "Are you okay?"

"Sore," he said, "and still a little confused." He looked around. "Allie? Lilith? The chalice? Did Jared do something to me?"

"Allie's fine," I told him. "You did it. You kept Lilith out of Allie."

"Then shouldn't I be insane? Am I insane?" he asked looking at Eric, who'd barreled in after me.

Eric shook his head. "I don't know, man. I always thought you were a little. But I think you came through the other side just fine."

"Why am I not dead or insane?" Stuart asked.

"Jared," I told him, "You were right that he did something. He saved you. He pulled you free. Allie's fine, and you're fine. It all worked out okay." My laughter sounded strange, and I realized I was probably in a bit of shock.

"Except for you being in a coma," I continued, words tumbling out of me. "That sucked. But you're here now.

Oh, God. We need to call a doctor? Shouldn't we call a doctor?"

I turned to Eric who nodded. "I'll do that right now," he said then pulled out his phone even as Allie returned with Jared, Laura, and Mindy. Word spread, and soon his small room was filled with almost everyone in the school, all talking at once about how pleased they were that Stuart was awake and did he remember anything about what he said when he was in the coma.

"Said?" He shook his head. "I don't know what you're talking about." He turned to look at Eric, who had turned away to speak into his phone, presumably with the medical team.

Stuart frowned. "How long have I been gone?"

"Almost three months," I told him.

He nodded slowly as if he couldn't quite process that. Then he started to look around the room. "Where's Timmy?"

Timmy! I was the worst mother in the world. Not only had I just slept with my ex-husband, but I didn't even know where my youngest child was in a gigantic house.

"He was here with Bruce and Ren earlier," Allie said with a nod toward Ren and Ana. "Actually, where's Bruce?"

No one answered, but in the silence I heard a small little, "Momma?"

I turned toward the connecting bedroom that would have been Nancy's quarters, realizing that of course he'd gone in there to play. The door was partially closed, so I pushed it wide open, intending to go scoop him up and deliver him to his daddy.

But when I did, I froze.

Because there was Timmy standing right next to Bruce, who was holding a deadly blade right at my little boy's neck.

14

"Allie comes with me or the brat dies," Bruce said, pulling my baby closer so that the point of the knife pressed against the soft skin of Timmy's neck. I held my breath, terrified, as my baby whimpered and called for me.

"Shut the hell up," Bruce snapped.

"It's okay, baby," I said gently to Timmy even as I moved to the side so that my body was blocking Allie. "Just stay very quiet and very still. Everything's going to be fine."

"Yeah, no," Bruce said. "I really don't think it is. Not unless Allie comes with me. If that happens, then your little dude will be just fine. If not, then I'll just leave you with sliced-and-diced little dude."

"Why?" I asked. "You had a chance here for a new start. You have talent and skill. You could have made a difference."

"Like you can do anything compared to her."

It took me a moment to realize he wasn't talking about Allie. He was talking about Lilith. I turned to face Eric, saw his grim expression, and knew he'd come to the same conclusion.

"You've spoken with her? How?"

"I don't have to tell you shit. I'm the one with the power. Ain't that right, Timmy-my-man?"

I kept my eyes on him, trying to tune out everyone else in the room. Trying to focus. To *think.*

"You're right," I said. "You have the power. Which is why you can answer my questions. You have the advantage."

"Damn right, I do. I'm her right-hand boy. They came to me. Told me. She chose *me.* And her deal is a hell of a lot sweeter than yours. Swords and knives and holy water? When she rewards me, I'll have power. Real power."

I shook my head. "She's manipulating you."

He shrugged. "Maybe. Maybe not. But she's going to be the queen of the world soon. I'm choosing my side. And you should, too," he added, turning his attention to Ren and Ana. "Didn't either of you learn anything during your time on the streets? No one helps you. No one wants you. You have to look out for yourself. *We* have to look out for ourselves."

I watched their face, Ana's full of shock. Ren's flat and emotionless.

"Come with me," Bruce urged. "We're the same breed, all of us. They don't care about us here. We're only scraps they picked up."

My heart sank as Ren took a step forward. I weighed my chances of rescuing Timmy as Bruce gloated. Not stellar, but it might be my best shot.

But then Ren's chin went up.

"You're wrong," he said, looking Bruce straight in the eye. I wanted to applaud him, but I didn't think it was the moment.

"I thought you were cool," Ana said, moving to stand beside Ren. "But you've been playing us since you killed Jessica, haven't you?"

Bruce smiled. "Jessica took one for the team, yeah."

"You're screwed up. How could you do this to a little boy?"

"I'm not doing anything to him. They are. All I want is Allie. She comes with, I let the kid go."

"You hurt him, and you are dead," Allie said, moving to my side. "You'd never get out of here. You know that, right?"

"Actually, I think I would," he said. "Guess which one of us is more likely to take that risk."

"What does she want?" Eric asked.

"Her," he said nodding to Allie. "Haven't you been paying attention?"

Allie turned to look at me, then Eric. She turned to look at everyone behind us. I did, too. Stuart was sitting on the side of his hospital bed now, his IV still attached, and his pale face lined with grief and fear. Laura stood with him, holding his hand. Mindy's eyes were on Allie, and I saw tears in her eyes as she shook her head, her mouth forming into the word *no*.

Beside her, Jared was holding onto the footrail of Stuart's bed, the metal denting under the force of his grip.

My whole body went numb as I realized that Mindy and Jared were one step ahead of me, and I turned back to Allie in shock.

My baby girl shrugged. "I have to," she said.

"We'll find another way."

Bruce snorted. "Yeah, thinking you won't. Not unless you want to sacrifice the Timster here. Whadda say? Should I filet him now?"

I wanted to scream at him. To tell him that he was wasting so much potential. But I knew it would be futile, and I'd only be risking his temper, and that meant risking Timmy's life.

"Allie." It was all I could say. All I could manage.

"You both know I'm right," she said, looking from me to her father. "That's why I'm here, isn't it? To fight demons? To help humanity? Isn't that what Father Donnelly said? I was bred for a purpose. So why not start at the top with Lilith? Why not start with saving my brother?"

"You're walking into a trap," I told her.

"I know." She turned and looked straight at Ren and Ana. "So I guess school's really open now, huh? And your first assignment is to figure out how to rescue me."

"This can't be happening," I said, pacing the entry hall thirty-one minutes later. "He can't have taken her."

Bruce had told us to wait in Stuart's room for thirty minutes, and we had, even with the *Forza* doctor having arrived to check Stuart out.

At exactly thirty minutes, all of us except Stuart had raced to the entry hall, only to see that there was no sign of them. Just the open gate at the driveway entrance, as if welcoming all demons, just so they could waltz in and rip my heart out.

"One of Lilith's minions must have waited for him in a car. He wouldn't drive himself—not with Allie in the car. He's not that stupid, and neither is Allie."

"I can't think," I said. "I can't even form thoughts. Eric..."

"I know," he said, pulling me close. I clung to him, craving the comfort until reality slapped me in the face. The reality of what just happened ... and the reality of what we'd done.

I pushed away, my body going hot with guilt as I saw Stuart and an elderly doctor standing on the stairwell landing, my husband weak and pale and thin.

"He's fine," the doctor said as I sprinted to him. "He'll need physical therapy, and he shouldn't strain himself, but I think he'll have a good recovery."

"Thank you."

"You don't remember me, but I treated many of your cuts and bruises in Rome back in the day. You, too," he said, nodding to Eric. "I moved back home to California last year, and Father Corletti asked if I wanted to come out of retirement." He glanced around, clearly assessing the situation. "I don't know what's going on here today, but I think I made the right choice saying yes."

"Doctor Carlton," I said. "I remember now."

"I can stay. Help."

I shook my head. "Thank you. But we're okay." I already felt overwhelmed by people and possibilities and the lack of a definitive plan. I didn't need another voice in my head. "But we'll call you if we need you. And see you when school officially starts."

I sounded so polished. So professional. But all I wanted to do was curl up in a ball and cry.

"I don't know much more than that doctor," Stuart said after Dr. Carlton left, "but you and Eric have been through worse."

I swallowed, my guilt rising again as he spoke so easily about Eric and me as a team.

But had to shake it off. This guilt. This fear. All of it. I had to push it away or else it would cloud my judgment.

"You'll get her back," Stuart continued. We'd walked down the stairs, and now he sat, two from the bottom. "And Allie's strong. She can take care of herself."

"Maybe," I said, sitting beside him, "but she still needs us. Timmy, too." Bruce had said he would see that Timmy was returned once he was certain that Allie couldn't escape. I hadn't liked those words or that plan, but considering the knife that I was certain he'd use, I also hadn't had a choice.

"Kate, is this still about Lilith? You don't have to

catch me up fully, but I need to know if that bitch is still screwing with our family."

"Yeah," I said. "It's about her."

He started to stand, his free hand reaching for the railing.

"Stuart, I don't think—"

I didn't get the words out before he collapsed, sliding back down and into Jared's arms, the latter having burst forward with preternatural speed to catch him.

"I think he's okay," Jared said. "Just weak."

"I'm fine," Stuart said, his voice thin and reedy.

"I'll take him back to the bed. Signora, could you watch him? Maybe feed him some broth after he naps?"

"*Si*," she said, then hurried to follow Jared upstairs.

I watched my husband taken from me and told myself I had to keep it together. My kids needed me. For that matter, so did the world. This was Lilith we were dealing with after all.

As everyone talked among themselves, the din of their voices marked with fear, I looked at Eric. My whole body hurt. Not physically, but my own fear felt like pain, and I wanted nothing more than to fall to the ground and curl into a little ball.

Get a grip, Kate. You've got this.

I repeated the words in my head, over and over, hoping that I would believe them. I didn't think that I ever truly would, but that didn't matter. I was going to act like they were true, and I was going to hope that, eventually, my pretend confidence would become real.

Eric came to me, then held out a hand to where I still

sat on the steps. He pulled me up and Laura rushed to my side, tears in her eyes.

"Do you have any idea how we're going to get them back?"

"She can fight," Marcus said. "She's a hell of a fighter."

"We will get her," Cutter added. "You just need to focus, Kate. You know you can do this."

I nodded, letting all of their words wash over me. I could do this. Allie could do this. It would all come out okay.

Somehow though I didn't believe it. Mostly, because I just didn't know how. Because I still couldn't see the plan.

"Kate." It was my name on Eric's lips, and suddenly I was thrust into the past. A past where we had gotten out of so many scrapes. A past where we had won, time and time again.

But it was also a past where we had lost our friends. Where we had seen those closest to us die at the hands of demons in cruel and horrible ways.

I looked away from him.

"Katherine Andrews, what do you think you are doing?"

I looked up to see Signora Micari hustling toward me with a tray of broth and juice. "This is not the young woman I knew. You would not give up so easily. And you would not let those around you give up so easily."

"I'm not," I said, feeling all of eleven again. "But it's my children. I don't know what to do."

"And because of that you should be stronger. You should know that we will find her. And we will find the little boy. Or we will die trying."

Not the most encouraging words, but they gave me strength. I nodded, as she came over to stand right in front of me.

"You are allowed to collapse because it is your children. But now you must put that away and get up. You must do what you can to help them, otherwise you have already failed them."

She was right. Dear God, she was right.

Slowly, I turned in a circle, looking around the room, my eyes landing first on Eric. "Okay, everybody," I said. "We need ideas. Lots of ideas."

In my fantasy world, someone blurted out a brilliant idea, and we swooped in for the rescue. Unfortunately, I wasn't living in a fantasy world. Everyone was quiet.

"First order of business is to find them," Eric finally said, clearly deciding to get the ball rolling since Ana and Ren hadn't jumped in.

"Lilith took her," Jared said, now back from getting Stuart settled. "We all agree on that, right? That's who Bruce was talking about. The *her* that he's serving."

"It must be."

"Well, then, he's probably taking her to wherever Celia is. That makes sense right? Lilith knows we don't know where that is, dammit. Despite me spending countless hours looking." He met my eyes, "I'm sorry I haven't found her yet. I'm sorry I haven't found them both."

"It's okay," I said. "At least we know what to rule out."

"They're probably close, right?" The timid voice came from Ana. "Doesn't make sense to go too far."

I turned to her, and I felt a smile touch my lips. "Yes," I said. "A-plus for reasoning."

"So we get a map," Jared said. "A big one. And we assess possible locations. I could try to track them—I know Allie's scent—but since they left in a car, I don't think it will work. My time's better spent helping brainstorm."

"Agreed," I said, then turned to look at everyone. "Research and thinking, people. We don't know anything except that we believe Jared's sister is close. We believe she's being held by Lilith's minions. As far as we know, Lilith is back in the ether."

I didn't mention Eddie's odd comment about a piece of Lilith being in Stuart or Allie. Since I'd never heard of anything like that, I assumed he was just spitballing, and I wasn't going to have everyone dig in on that research unless Eddie told me it was real.

"Jared's had a few visions of his sister, too, so he can give you more details, but the big picture is that she's being held somewhere with crystal walls. Possibly a vault. The telepathy between vampires can't go through crystal, so we know that's how Lilith was holding her. But she let Celia reach out once or twice just to yank Jared's chain. Hopefully, something he saw will give us a starting point."

I nodded for Jared to take over.

"I didn't see much. The walls seem to be made of stone. There were windows, but they were all up high. Celia said she was buried, which I assume means that whatever room they kept her in was an underground vault.

"Once, I thought I heard the howl of a wolf or a bobcat. I couldn't tell. And one time, Celia spun around and told me that she was crazy-dancing in the light. By that time, she was really losing it, so I don't know if that's important, but that's how she said it."

"I'm really sorry," Ana said. "You must be so worried."

His mouth twisted a bit, as if he was fighting tears, and he nodded silently before saying, "Yeah. We were always close. And once we were turned—well, she's lived over a hundred years now, but she looks ten. I take care of her. Or I did. Before Lilith's people took her."

"Have you had a vision since what happened at the Stone Table?" I asked. I realized I'd never asked that before. I'd assumed that he had since he was still looking for her, but I didn't know for sure.

He shook his head. "No." He turned to look at Ana and Ren. "Lilith was blackmailing me. Pave the way for her to get into Allie, and I'd get my sister back. And I was going to—I really was. But then—"

"What?" Ana asked, her eyes wide.

"He saved Stuart instead," I said, when it was clear Jared wasn't going to answer. Stuart had intended to sacrifice himself to save Allie. And so Jared had saved Stuart. Because Stuart had saved the girl that Jared loved.

170

"She must be really pissed at you," Ren said. "Lilith, I mean."

"Yeah," Jared said. "I'm hoping she's pissed enough that she's keeping Celia from me. I think I'd know if my sister were dead. But ... Anyway, it's our best lead. Wherever she's keeping—or kept—Celia, that's probably where Allie is, too."

He looked so broken, that I told everyone to go get busy thinking and researching, and that we'd reconvene in an hour. Jared started to follow, but I caught up with him. "You okay?"

He shrugged, then took a seat on the staircase. I joined him, sitting silently and looking at the ornate tiles that decorated this grand entranceway.

This stately old mansion had once been the home of Theophilus Monroe, the black sheep of his family who had been deep into the occult. So deep, that he'd meticulously incorporated demonic symbols throughout the place. Including, I assumed, the tiles I was looking at.

When I'd first suggested we use the mansion as a school, I assumed Father Corletti would look at the history and say no. But then Father explained that we could turn the darkness around. Bring it into the light. Take away the power of the demons and make this place a home filled with goodness and hope and a passion for fighting for the right.

Now, I looked at all those symbols on the floor and twined into the railings, and I hoped that he was right. I hoped that this house was imbued with good. With the power to help us get through this.

Because right then, all I could think about, was the time that Lilith—in the form of that bitch Nadia—had made it through the doors, and had almost taken Eric from me.

After a moment, Jared offered me a thin smile. "I don't think it helps, but I do understand how you feel now about Timmy."

I thought of Celia, and nodded. "And Allie?" I asked.

He didn't pretend to misunderstand. "I don't know how you feel about her leaving. Going with him. Risking her life for her little brother. Pride, I assume. Fear, I think. I don't know, because I'm not her mother." He'd been talking to the floor. Now he turned to face me. "I don't have the same kind of love for her that you do."

"But you do love her."

"I do," he said. "I truly do. Does that bother you?"

"It scares me," I admitted.

"Because I'm so much older."

"Yes. And that pesky fact that you're a vampire."

"You don't trust me?"

I shook my head. "That came out wrong. Of course I trust you."

"Good. Because from what I understand, one of the men you're in love with has a demon inside him that managed to get out not that long ago. Or had a demon. Honestly it's all a bit confusing. "

"Sounds like Allie's told you our entire family history."

He shrugged. "I hope that's okay. We've been talking a lot. She's a lot older than sixteen, you know."

"And yet she's really not."

"Do you think I don't know that, too?"

"Do you?"

"I'm not going to walk away," he said. "But I'm also not going to push her. Nothing's happened between us if that's what you're wondering. And nothing will until she's ready. If she's ever ready."

Since I wasn't sure what the appropriate mom-answer was, I stayed silent.

He clasped his hands together and put them between his knees as he looked down. "The truth is, I don't think she feels the same way about me. She *thinks* she loves me, but I don't know what that means to her. She's focused, our Allie. She understands what's been put on her shoulders. I want to take part of that burden from her. I want to help her. But I don't know that she's ever going to let me. She's remarkable, Kate." He tilted his head toward me. "From what I've seen, she got that from you."

"I like you, Jared. And for what it's worth, I think you're good for her. And I think she really loves you. In whatever way a sixteen-year-old girl loves the first boy that she's fallen for. And you are the first boy. So be careful with her heart, please. And, like you said, give her space. She has a lot on her platter."

"Yes, ma'am," he said, and I laughed.

"Considering you're older than me, I think we can dispense with the ma'am."

"Do you really want to be thinking about the fact that I'm older than you and Allie put together?"

We shared a grin, and I shook my head. "No. Probably not." My heart twisted. "Right now, though, none of it really matters, does it?"

"We're going to find her, Kate. I promise you, somehow we're going to find her."

Two hours later, his words were still circling in my head, but we seemed to be no closer to finding her. My phone rang and I snatched it up, though why I was so eager, I didn't know. Everyone was here, and it wasn't as if Lilith was going to make a phone call.

Then again, I supposed Bruce might. It wasn't Bruce, though. The call was Rita's daughter, Fran.

"Fran? I'm a little busy. What's up?"

"I'm at your house," my friend said, sounding a bit bewildered. "And I have Timmy."

15

"W ait," I said. "You have Timmy?"

Jared reached over and took my hand. I squeezed it hard.

"Yeah. And I have to be honest, Kate. I'm a little worried about Allie. If she's dating the guy who was in the backseat—"

"Fran, what happened?"

"Oh." I heard the surprise in her voice at my tone, but I didn't apologize. I just needed to know. "Well, Elena and I were on our way over to borrow your bucket of Legos. Eddie said you wouldn't mind. You don't mind, do you?"

"Of course not. What happened?"

"I'd just pulled into the driveway and was getting out of the car, when they pulled up against the curb. Allie's windows rolled down and some guy leaned across to say that he and Allie were babysitting Timmy, but that they were supposed to drop him off with Eddie. Is that right?"

I looked at Jared, who nodded. "Yeah," I said. "Absolutely right. Why did you say you were worried about Allie?"

"A bad vibe, I guess. I asked her, and she said she was fine. Just tired. But, I don't know. Now I feel like I could have called you right then. Honestly, Kate, I think she might have been drinking."

"But you took Timmy? And he's okay?"

"Yes, of course, he's fine."

You didn't happen to see the direction they left in, did you?"

"They took the north exit out of the subdivision, or at least it looked like they were going to. Towards the hills, not the city. Kate, seriously, you're worrying me."

"I swear it's fine. I'll be right over to get him."

"Eddie's here. I'm sure he'll—"

"I'll be right there," I repeated, then hung up. I stood and raced up the stairs, eager to tell Stuart we had Timmy back.

"I'm going to get him now," I said, a moment later as I held his hand. He was back in bed, looking bone-tired. But he was awake and alive. And so was our little boy.

Finally, things were starting to look up.

"I love you," I said, bending over to kiss his cheek. "I have to go now."

"No, you don't," Eric said from the doorway.

"What are you talking about? I have to go get Timmy."

"Jared texted me. This is incredible news, but he's

safe with Eddie. And you, Kate, are a wreck. I don't want you behind the wheel. Not right now."

"Are you insane? I am going to go see my little boy."

"I'll go."

I turned to see Laura in the doorway. For such a big mansion, word traveled fast.

"Not alone you aren't." I wasn't going to argue with the fact that I was too rattled to drive. Eric was right. But there was no way I was letting Laura go out on those streets by herself. For all I knew someone was lying in wait at the house.

"I'll go with her," Cutter said. "We'll call you as soon as we see him. Okay?"

I hesitated, then nodded. "Okay. Okay, this is good. This is a start. Go," I said. "Please, go now."

They did, and I let myself sag against the doorframe, Fran's words running back through my head. "He drugged her," I said. "Fran said she sounded strange. Like she'd been drinking."

"He doesn't want her to be able to defend herself," Jared said, joining us in the room.

I looked to Eric again. "Why did he let Timmy go?"

"I don't know. He probably thought that Allie would be more cooperative if her little brother wasn't in danger."

I nodded. That made sense. But still... "Maybe he's not as far gone as he seems," I said. "Maybe he was willing to take Allie in order to get whatever Lilith's minions are promising him, but he wasn't willing to hurt a child in the process."

"It's possible," Eric said. "But I don't think so. I heard his words. I saw his eyes. I think the Bruce we brought into this school was an act. I think that boy's been damaged for a very long time."

"There's always hope," I said.

"And that's why I love you," Eric said, with everyone in the room listening. Not that our past was a secret. But right then, after everything that had happened, it felt like a flashing neon light.

I took Stuart's hand again and twined our fingers. "Whatever his reason, it gives us an advantage. Eventually, the drugs will wear off. Probably faster than he expects. And she'll be able to defend herself, right? Allie's come so far, of course she'll be okay."

Eric drew in a breath, then slowly let it out. "Kate, I know you're scared. I am too, but you have to think of this as a mission."

His words were like a slap in the face. But he was right, and it was a slap I needed. I wasn't acting like the Hunter I was trained to be. I was acting like a mom, spinning what-ifs about how her kid would handle herself. All well and good if I was a mom sending her daughter off to prom.

But in this situation, acting like that mom could get my daughter killed.

I let go of Stuart's hand, then moved to the doorway. I hit the emergency button by the door, knowing it would call everyone in the building to this location. Then I leaned against the doorframe and waited.

Less than two minutes later, I stood in that doorway

and looked at the faces now gathered in Stuart's room and briefed them on the situation.

"And that means you all have jobs. For that matter, you all have the same job. I want suggestions from all of you on how we can find her, and I want them now. And when I say *all*, I mean everybody including you two," I added, pointing to Ren and Ana.

Everyone stood silent.

I held out my hands. "Well? Start throwing things out. I don't care how stupid. This is brainstorming. We need to start formulating a plan."

I glanced sideways at Eric and shook my head in mock disapproval. He smiled and nodded. Apparently I was back on the right track.

Ren thrust his hand up.

"You can just call it out, Ren. No need for propriety."

"What about Quiric? He might know."

"But why would he tell?" Jared asked.

"He reveres Allie, right? She shut that gate thing, didn't she? That free pass thing? He'd help her, wouldn't he?"

"And that is the way we do it," I said. "Excellent work, Ren. Volunteers?"

Marcus and Eliza both raised their hands along with Jared. "Good. Ren's in charge. Pick your team."

Ren's eyes went wide. "Me?"

"It was your plan. You lead it."

Slightly behind him, Eliza and Marcus looked at each other. I caught Marcus's eye, and he nodded, silently telling me that he would take over if need be. But I had a feeling Ren was up to the challenge.

"Um, Marcus and Eliza," Ren said, then cleared his throat. "And, yeah, sorry, Jared. But you're not going."

The vampire was at his side in a heartbeat. "Excuse me?"

"Ren already gave you an answer," Marcus said. "And it was the right one. We'll have a better shot of getting more information—assuming there is more—if you're not there. Not you or Kate or Eric. You're too close."

I watched as Jared seethed, his fangs visible.

"He's right," I said, and Jared turned dark eyes on me. "He's right," I repeated.

"Fine," he said, then was on the other side of the room before I could blink. Drama, maybe, but I gave him points. This was the kind of passion and protectiveness I wanted to see in a guy who was dating my daughter. And the speed and strength were a bonus, too.

After the Quiric team headed out, I dismissed the others, telling them we'd gather again in an hour, and to keep brainstorming.

"Not you," I said, as Eric started to pass. "Eddie said something to me the other day and, oh, hang on."

I pulled out my phone and texted Laura, asking her to bring Eddie back with her when she and Cutter brought Timmy.

"I'll ask him when he gets here, but in the meantime, he said something to me, and I'm not sure if it's legit or if he was just making stuff up."

"I'm listening."

We were still in Stuart's room, and we sat in the two chairs by the bed so that Stuart could listen, too.

"It was the first time that Stuart talked," I said, noticing the way Stuart's brow furrowed with that comment. "We were at the house, remember? And Eddie said something about how maybe he had a piece of Lilith in him. A piece. Is that even possible? Can a demon—or a High Demon—split themselves like that?"

"Like mercury," Eric said. "And then eventually the two blobs go back together?"

"You're talking science. I'm just asking if it's a thing."

"Not that I've heard of," Eric said. "Demonic essence is incorporeal, obviously, but my understanding is that it's still a whole entity. Then again, Eddie's seen a lot of things in his time. Maybe there are exceptions."

Stuart lifted his hand, catching my attention. "Did you just say that there's a piece of the demon Lilith in me?"

"Eddie was just running through ideas," I told him. "We practically drenched you in holy water. You're fine. You're fine," I repeated as much to soothe him as myself.

"But why did you think there was a demon in me at all?"

"You said things," I told him gently. "Cryptic things. Do you remember any of them? Maybe you saw something while you were unconscious? Did you have visions? Maybe you saw something to suggest where Lilith might be?"

I waited for answers. For him to have an *aha* moment and tell me that he pictured a tacky mansion where Lilith was sitting in a gilt chair in a ball gown with her legs crossed, just waiting for us to enter and be struck down.

Of course he didn't say that. Instead he said, "I don't remember any of it. I don't remember anything at all. There was nothing after the table, except for Jared. I remember him pulling me away. Then there was nothing. Then I woke up. It felt like no time had passed at all." He looked between us. "What did I say?"

"The first time you said something about Allie. You said *Be careful* and *Allie.* Then you paused before saying *isn't.* Does that mean anything to you?"

"No, but it sounds like I was telling her to be careful, and that something wasn't safe."

"Yeah, well, I guess you were right about that," I said, as Eric reached for my hand. I tugged it away, clasping my hands together in my lap.

"You were right about the other, too," Eric said. "You said *rat.*"

"A traitor," Stuart said. "That boy."

"Bruce. Yeah." I reached for my husband's hand. "How about that? Do you remember that?"

"No. None of it."

"You were warning us," I said. "And we had no idea."

"How could you have?" Stuart asked. "The way you described it sounds like nonsense." He was speaking slowly, his throat still raw from lack of use. "That's over, right? It was something that happened in the coma because I'd been hit by some mystical whammy."

"Who knows," Eric said. "But it's a good guess. The few cases I found that seemed similar to yours—and basically there were none—ended when the patient woke up. Or died," he added with a shrug.

"You found more cases?"

"Only one," Eric told me. "A woman in the sleep of death, they called it. But she woke up after a month. No more cryptic sleepwalking."

"Too bad," Stuart said, looking at me. "As strange as the idea is, it would be nice to finally be some real help around here."

Except for Stuart, who was stretched out on a sofa we'd pulled into the room, we were all gathered around the dining table finishing up another update and brainstorming session when Laura and Cutter returned with Timmy, Eddie, Rita, Fran, and four-year-old Elena.

"Momma! Momma!" Timmy called.

"Baby!" I raced forward then scooped him into my arms, relishing the way he hugged me so tight he could probably break a rib.

"I went with Allie and Bruce and his friend in the car. Bruce played a Bad Guys game."

"I know. He's very good at that game."

"Miss Fran gave me ice cream."

"Lucky for you. Did you bring me any?" I looked at his hands as if searching for a cone.

"Mo*mma*. That's silly. Ice cream melts."

"Good point." I gave him another squeeze, not

wanting to put him down, but knowing I had to. "Guess what else? I have a big surprise for you."

"Yay! What is it?"

I turned him around to see Stuart, pretty sure that he hadn't overheard that his dad had awakened in all the commotion with Bruce.

"Daddy!"

I put him down, and he ran to Stuart as I cried for him to be gentle because Daddy still didn't feel well.

"Okay, Momma," he said, climbing up on the couch to snuggle with his father, who winced a little through his smile.

It's fine, he mouthed to me. *It's great.*

My youngest now safe with his dad, I took a moment to savor, then turned to Fran, Eddie, and Rita.

"What's all the talk about Bruce playing the bad guy?" Eddie asked.

"They all insisted on coming," Laura called from where she'd already settled in at the table, her laptop still there from the morning.

"It's fine," I said. "And, yeah. We had an incident with Bruce. Fran, I owe you pretty much everything."

"I didn't do a thing except take him when offered. And sorry again about just barging in, but we thought we might be able to help."

I was about to tell her we were fine—because how could I tell her we were knee deep in demons—when she continued.

"I mean, I figure you need all the help you can get if you're fighting a demon like Lilith."

I gaped at her, and she shrugged. "Oh, come on, Kate. My mom told me what happened with Nancy. And I've overheard some of the stories that Eddie's told her, too."

I shot a glare at Eddie, who only shrugged. Beside him, Rita flashed a smile. "You know how hard it is to keep secrets from family. And now that Fran and Elena are living with me, they hear so much." She leaned closer. "D.I.V.O.R.C.E."

I turned to Fran. "Sorry. I hadn't heard."

"Don't be sorry. It's good, believe me. Although money is tight, so I'm not much help on her rent. Plus I'm cramping my mom's style."

"Mommy!" Elena tugged at Fran's hand, demanding attention. "Can I play with Timmy?"

I glanced over to Stuart, who nodded. "Sure," I told Elena. "Just play quietly. Mr. Stuart isn't feeling very good."

She nodded, then bounced off.

"I really would like to help," Fran said. "I know you probably think it's a lot for me to absorb in one day, but I swear it's not. I've noticed the same things around town my mom has. And you have to admit you stand out a little bit, Kate, especially having gotten into all those fights."

"And here I thought I was so stealthy."

"I know there's not a whole lot I can do, but Mom told me about Nancy. I thought maybe I could take over that job, but since Stuart's awake, I guess you don't need anyone watching him sleep anymore."

"We don't," I said. "Thankfully, he's doing great."

"I'm really happy to hear that even though I guess it means you don't need me. Unless there's something menial I can help with. I really do want to help if I can. Eddie told me what happened with Allie. I can't even imagine."

I had texted him, of course. Telling him Laura and Cutter were on the way, and giving him the full story.

I was about to tell her I couldn't think of a thing. Then I saw Timmy and Elena playing beside Stuart's sofa, where he'd drifted off into a nap.

"Actually, Fran, I do have a job for you..."

16

Fortunately, Fran thought that the idea of playing daycare provider for Timmy at the school sounded like a great idea. Apparently, she'd lost her job when the insurance company she worked at downsized. Now, she assured me, she was excited to start down a new path. "Especially if you'll teach me the demony stuff. And if I can watch Elena at the same time."

Not only did I agree, but I offered her one of the staff bedrooms so that she and Elena could move in. The same style I had, with a bedroom for her, and a smaller attached nursery for Elena.

"Not necessarily the safest job or living arrangement," I warned her. "But it's yours if you want it."

I was thrilled that she did, and even though Laura pouted and announced that she was being tossed aside for a new best friend, I knew that Laura was thrilled with the arrangement, too.

"I have no idea how I'll put this on my resume," Fran said with a laugh.

"*Forza West*, a private boarding academy for K-12. Stuart did all the paperwork. If anyone looks closely, we're just a school."

Fran insisted on starting immediately so that I could focus on Lilith and Allie. So while she went upstairs with the kids, the rest of us continued with the research and thinking. Which, honestly, had never been my strong suit. I was much better at action. Right then, though, I had no action to take, and the lack of either a mission or answers was starting to drive me crazy. My baby was out there, and it felt like I was getting nowhere.

I frowned, looking around the dining room for Eddie, but he was nowhere to be found. "I'm going to go find him," I told Eric. "I need to know about this partial demon thing."

I headed upstairs first, since I knew that Rita had gone up with Fran. He wasn't with them—though Fran did tell me that Rita was going to watch the kids while she went home to pack a few thing—so I went next to my bedroom to check on Stuart.

He wasn't there, and I cringed, realizing he'd probably gone back to the room with the temporary hospital bed.

Sure enough, there he was, stretched out on the mattress, his eyes closed.

"Are you awake?" I whispered.

"I'm here," he said, opening his eyes and sitting up. "Didn't seem like I was much help."

"Right now, the best thing you can do is rest."

As he nodded, I moved closer, thinking I was going to tell him everything. But when I reached his bed, all I said was, "I love you."

"I know. I love you, too."

"You don't have to stay in here, you know. We have a bedroom. With a real bed. You don't have an IV anymore and no one needs to keep a constant eye."

He studied my face. "You were really worried."

"Of course I was. I still am. You look so tired considering you've been sleeping for months."

"The doctor said that was normal. Lots of vitamin packed shakes, then vitamin packed food and I'll improve daily."

"Good. Want to see our room?"

He smiled and his eyes crinkled in that way they had when we'd first started dating. "Yeah. I think I would."

I helped him out of bed, then walked him out of the room and over to ours. "Fran's moving in," I said. "She's going to be our child care person. Did you know she got divorced?"

"I've been a little absent."

"Right. Yeah, well I didn't know. Nine weeks ago. I'm a terrible friend."

"I think you were preoccupied with other things," he said. "Part of which was me. Sorry about that. Between me being absent and you trying to get the school up and running, I know you must have been going crazy."

"I was, but it's okay. Right now I just..." I shook my head. "I can't stop being terrified. I keep telling myself I need to stop being terrified. That I need to think and do my job. But I can't seem to help myself even though I know that Allie needs Clear-headed Mom. Not Terrified Mom."

"You'll find her."

I drew in a breath. "I know. I have to. I can't even consider any other outcome."

As he takes my hand, I shake my head, clearing away my thoughts. "At any rate," I said, trying to sound chipper, "I'm glad Fran's going to be here. It's nice having my friends know the truth." I looked up at him. "I remember how nice it was when you learned the truth."

I think about the secret. The truth I need to reveal. Now would be the perfect moment. But I can't seem to do it.

Instead, I clear my throat, then nod toward our bed. "This is where we live now."

"What happened to the house?"

"Eddie's living there with Eric. But he's engaged to Rita, and he wants Eric to move in here so she can move in and they can be alone." I grinned. "Mostly, I think he believes we'll be safer if Eric is on the premises. Honestly, I'm not sure that's such a good idea."

I think Stuart will agree, and I can suggest to Eric he live elsewhere. But Stuart only nodded and said, "Eddie's right. Eric's one hell of a fighter. And unless you did a significant remodel of this place, there's plenty of bedrooms for all the instructors, and plenty of dorm rooms for the students."

"No, you're right about that. There's tons of room."

I shrugged. "It's just..." I trailed off, not knowing how I was going to finish that sentence. I knew I should tell him the truth, but I also knew that wasn't going to happen. Not right then, anyway.

"I get it. This school is supposed to be your baby, and if Eric is here, then maybe it will feel more like a shared venture. But I think he'll give you your space. We've had our differences, but he's a good guy."

"Yeah," I said. "He is."

I moved closer and kissed him gently on the cheek, feeling like a completely horrible person. "Anyway, you like the room?"

He turned in a circle, taking in the bare walls and the plain dresser. I never had been one for decorating, and I'd been a little busy.

"We'll work on it," he said, then gave me a sideways hug as he laughed. "I love you."

"I love you too," I said, meaning every word. But knowing that sometimes love could be more complicated than you wanted it to be.

I started out the door, intending to let him rest while I went back to work trying to find my daughter.

"Katherine," he said, his voice sounding deeper and a bit melodious.

I turned, confused, to find him standing and staring glassy-eyed into space. "Stuart?"

"The ruby can reveal her."

"What?"

But he didn't say anything else. Instead, his legs gave

out and he tumbled to the floor. I rushed to his side as he opened his eyes.

"Kate?" His voice was perfectly normal. "What happened?"

"You spoke again. You don't remember?"

He shook his head.

"You said *the ruby can reveal her.*" Do you know what that means?

"No. No idea at all."

"Me neither," I said, helping him up and into bed. "But I think you may have just helped again. At least, I hope so.

When I stepped out of the bedroom, Eric was standing there, leaning against the rail that overlooked the first floor.

"Don't you have research to do?" I asked as we walked down the stairs.

"I assume you talked to Stuart."

I paused. "No. I didn't."

"Why not?"

"I just didn't," I snapped, continuing to the entry hall. "We can talk about this later. Right now, we have more important things."

"The pieces of Lilith. I've been looking into that. So far, nothing."

I nodded. "And what Stuart said. We didn't *talk*, but he did. He had another episode."

"Really." It was his turn to pause. "Was he awake?"

"Yeah. And then he was—I don't know—reciting. He said that the ruby will reveal her. We need to know what that means."

"If it means anything."

"You think it doesn't?"

Eric shook his head. "Actually, my guess is it will be important. But we need to be prepared for disappointment."

"But you'll research it?"

"Of course." He paused long enough to send a text.

"Assigning one of the students?"

"Texting *Forza*. We need an answer fast."

I nodded. "We should mention it to Eddie, too. If we ever find him."

It took a while, but we finally found him in the kitchen trying to finagle cannolis from Signora Micari.

"Take this beast out of my kitchen," she said. "He is a human vacuum."

We bribed Eddie with two of the treats, then dragged him to the dining table which, at the moment, was only occupied by Jared who was reading a book that looked ancient, smelled musty, and seemed to be written in another language.

"Anything?"

He shook his head. "I'm trying to figure out if there are ways to enhance a vampire's telepathic powers. Get through to Celia and maybe get more information on their location. Nothing so far."

"Good plan, though. Keep looking. Will we bother you?"

He shook his head, but didn't look up from the book.

"Heard Father Donnelly was here," Eddie said, cream on his upper lip.

"I'll tell you all about it later," I promised. "The big news flash is that we really are related. And my ancestors and Eric's accidentally conjured gates to hell."

"Heh. Related, eh. Don't go trusting him. You listen to me, girlie."

"I know." But despite Eddie's years of warning me off Father Donnelly, I had to admit that the more I learned, the more I wanted to know. And that meant I was going to have to get to know him better.

But not right now. Now, I needed to focus. "Stuart said something," I told him. "Do you know anything about demons and rubies?"

His bushy brows drew together. "Say again?"

"Stuart had another trance thing. He said that a ruby would reveal her. Does that mean anything to you?"

Slowly, Eddie shook his head. Then he looked at Eric. "A job for the librarian, I'd say."

"I'm on it."

"It was just a thought," I said. "What I really wanted to ask you about was the thing you said about pieces. You said something about how Lilith might have been partially inside Allie or Stuart, remember? That day at my house after Stuart spoke the first time."

"I remember, girlie. Nothing wrong with my memory."

"You never explained how it was possible."

"I don't think it is," Eric said. "Trust me when I say that I've done a bit of research on High Demons moving into a living body, and there aren't any *Forza* accounts of that happening without consent. And in all my reading, I don't remember seeing anything about a partial inhabitation. As far as I've seen, there's no indication that a High Demon can get—and stay in—a living human. Even if they went the possession route, they'd burn out the flesh in under a minute."

"Yeah, well that's the thing," Eddie said.

"What is? I asked.

"It might be bullshit. Or it might be our best line of research. And I'm not surprised you haven't read about it. As far as I know, *Forza* doesn't have any experience with this."

"What are you talking about?" Eric asked.

"This is something you learned about after you left *Forza*," I said. "Isn't it?"

Eddie had a falling out with *Forza* many decades ago. He'd become a rogue Demon Hunter and from what he's told me, he had quite a few adventures.

"Are you saying that you've seen a partial inhabitation?" Eric asked. "If there's still a piece of her in our realm...."

"There's no chalice stone," I reminded him.

"No, but Quiric said something about Solomon's Stone, right?"

"It's destroyed," I said. "It doesn't exist."

"Maybe Lilith doesn't know that," Eric said.

"Or maybe she has another plan," I countered.

"Do you want to hear about the partial inhabitation or not?" Eddie asked, glaring at us in turn.

"Yes," I said, shooting Eric a sideways glance. "Very much."

"I was in Europe," he began, "and I met another rogue hunter. Apparently, he was on the run. He'd managed to reverse a demonic ritual to bring some High Demons over from a hell dimension. They got here, and he sent them right back packing. I don't know the details. At this point, the guy had pretty much lost it."

"Well, that sounds promising," Eric said.

Eddie shot him a scowl, and Eric cleared his throat, then said, "Please keep going. What happened with the rogue?"

"Like I said, he reversed the ritual, and was feeling pretty smug."

"But?"

"But one stayed behind," Eddie said. "My friend didn't realize until later, of course. But somehow he learned that the High Demon had left a piece of itself behind."

"That's all you know?" Eric said. "Unless you have more details, that's useless."

"Steady on, boy. That's not all. He killed the host—and the High Demon was gone. *Poof* gone. Not popped into another body gone. But gone back to the source demon. So once you find this host, all you have to do is kill it."

"Well, that's good news," I said. "But how do we know the host didn't have to be complicit. High Demons can totally share with a human if they find one to time-share. Although, then they have to fight the human's will."

"I think you just answered that question yourself, girlie."

I looked at Eric, confused, then saw realization strike his face. "They didn't move into living flesh. They moved into another demon."

"But that makes no sense," I said. "Regular demons move into dead humans as a matter of course. High Demons can do it, too, but they can't stay long. They'd just burn through the body. Maybe doing it partially changes that, but then they reduce their power, right?"

"Maybe sometimes it's worth it," Eric said.

"Like when you're thinking there might be a human body who can host a High Demon even without consent. Because then you use a ritual like the one with the chalice stone, and the complete High Demon swoops in to take over that special human's body."

"A human like Allie," he said.

"Eric..."

He nodded. "I know."

"How are we going to find this bit of Lilith? She could be in any demon anywhere."

"No," Eric said. "She'd want to stay close to us. Especially since she needs Allie."

"So this demon she's in will be holed up wherever Allie is hidden."

"Possibly. Unless she doesn't have full autonomy. It's only a piece of her. What if the host doesn't even know?"

"No," I said. "We don't have time for more questions. We need answers. We need to know—*Oh.*" I looked at them both. "I may be wrong, but unless you have a better idea, I know the perfect host. Someone we'd never even think of. And someone our students are with right now. Eric," I said. "We need to go."

"Quiric," Eric said. "Oh, hell."

We stood, ready to sprint out of there just as Signora Micari entered with a plate of cannolis. "Oh, you are going so soon?"

"They are," Eddie said. "I'll take another."

"Save a few for us," Eric told her. "With luck, we'll want to celebrate." His phone rang, and he glanced at the display, then to me. "Father Corletti."

"Tell him we're in a hurry."

He put it on speaker. "Father, we need—"

"You are correct," Father interrupted. "It is not a common thing, but we do have documentation of a ruby being used to identify those in whom a demon hides."

"How?" I asked.

"Once touched by the host, the ruby turns black."

I looked at Eric. "We need to find a ruby. Like right now."

"Oh, Katherine, you will take mine, yes?" The

signora tugged a long necklace from her body to reveal a gold setting with a large ruby. It was so big I wished we could just whack it into pieces to issue to everyone at the school. Maybe then we'd find the demon faster.

Hopefully the demon was Quiric, and no more searching would be necessary.

"Thank you," I said as she handed it to me. "But are you sure?"

"My whole life, I have helped with this battle. Of course, I am sure. Go. You are closer to finding our Allie. Now go."

"Damn it, why are none of them answering their phones?" I am definitely not one for technology, but it does piss me off when people have the little devices, and don't use them.

"It's okay," Eric said. "They're fine. They're together. Marcus and Eliza can handle themselves. And Ren and Ana both seem sharp."

"We still need to find them," I snapped. I told myself I didn't need to worry. Quiric wasn't on Lilith's side. But what if she was sneakily inside him? What if that meant she could turn him on a dime. "Dammit," I said, when Ana's phone went to voicemail.

"It's okay, Kate. I know where they are."

"You know where they are? Why didn't you just tell me that? For that matter, how do you know?"

"Location services. I made all the students turn it on."

"Oh. Okay. I was expecting some sort of mystical answer. But that works."

He shot me a grin. "Sometimes the easiest way is the best way."

"Some people would say the mystical way is the easiest way."

"But not you."

"No, not me. My way has always been the fighting way."

To be honest. In the demon hunting world there's a lot that's mystical, but very little that's the kind of magic you see on TV. Which meant we couldn't just do a spell and suddenly know where Quiric was located.

It would be nice if real life worked like fiction, but that never seems to happen. I guess that's why they call it real life.

"We'll be there in about ten," Eric said. He looked sideways at me. "Time enough to have that chat?"

"I'm not ready to have that chat."

"For the record, I don't regret what happened."

"What part of I'm not ready do you not understand?"

"And I'm not upset that Stuart is awake."

I turned in my seat and glared at him. "Eric. I mean it. Not now."

"I'm serious, too," he said. "I'm happy that you have him back. For him being alive and okay, not to mentioned enhanced with a touch of the oracle."

"Eric, just stop."

"And," he added, in a gentler tone. "I understand that this whole thing is confusing for you."

I sagged back in my seat, giving in. "Nothing has changed," I said. "Yes, we got physical, and yes, it didn't suck. But nothing has changed."

"Didn't suck. That's high praise indeed."

"Eric, don't you dare make a joke out of this."

"I'm not. I swear."

"It didn't suck at all, and you know it. Farthest thing from it. Which is only one part of why this is so hard."

"I know," he said. "I really do."

"And I mean it when I say that nothing has changed. You already knew that I still loved you. For that matter, Stuart knew it too. I made sure he knew it."

"Look at me," he said as he stopped at a light.

I did, almost sliding into those familiar eyes.

"I get it. I do understand. And I believe you when you say that nothing has changed. But that's from your perspective, Kate. From mine, it's everything. Whether or not I get to keep it, or if I just got to glimpse it, I don't know. That depends on you."

I stayed silent.

"Kate?" I turned to face him, but once again I said nothing.

"Will you tell him?"

I shifted so I could look out the window. "I have to."

"But you haven't yet."

"He just woke up from a coma and Allie is missing. Somehow the timing seemed wrong. But I will tell him,"

I said. Because the more I said it, the more I would start to believe it. I couldn't keep this from him.

Eric sighed. "Right when I was starting to get along with the guy, too. Guess I burned everything to the ground."

I felt the weight of his words through my body. "Eric, I am sorry. And I know it affects you too, but this isn't a secret I can keep." Even as I said the words though, I wished they weren't true. I wanted to keep this a secret. I wanted this to be the final ending with Eric, something Stuart didn't need to know anything about.

But that wasn't the way the rules worked. I needed to tell him. But whether I needed to tell him because I truly believed he needed to know or because I needed to clear my conscience, I really wasn't sure. And I wondered if it was fair to tell him if the latter was my true reason.

"You do what you have to do, Kate. But speaking of secrets, I've never made it a secret that this is a fight I want to win. I didn't lose you fair and square. I lost you because the universe screwed us up. Because the demons got between us. Because I was dead when I wasn't supposed to be.

Stuart got in the middle of that, and I'm sorry about that. But this is a fight I want to win. Your mine, Katie. And you always will be."

I closed my eyes, my throat dry. I could hear the emotion in his voice. It was running through me, burning me. And the truth was, I wanted it, too. The bigger truth was that I wanted it all. At the end of the day I was greedy. I was greedy and confused and lost.

"Can we just..."

He held up a hand. "We're here." I looked out the window, and saw why he had stopped so suddenly. He had driven right into an alley. I could see Quiric clearly.

And he had Ren pressed against a wall, his hand around the boy's throat.

17

I was out of the van before Eric had even killed the engine, my stiletto in my hand. I lifted it, saw I had a clear shot to Quiric's eye, and snapped my wrist to send my blade flying.

"No!" Eliza leaped forward, knocking Quiric and Ren to the ground as my stiletto smashed with a *thwang* against the brick wall.

"What the hell?" I called out at the same time that Marcus shouted, "We're training! Just training!"

I stopped cold, realizing the mistake I'd almost made. "Teaching moment," I muttered, making a mental note to turn this into class material. But later.

Right now I was just irritated.

"Explain," I demanded as they stood up, brushing themselves off. Eric had reached me, and didn't look any happier than I felt. "You're here to get information. About my daughter. Who's missing. Not play tackle with a demon."

Eliza grimaced. "Sorry. Truly. He doesn't know anything else about Celia's location." She looked between me and Eric. "I believe him. And then—"

Quiric held up a hand, cutting her off. "There is urgency in your eyes. Why do you seek me?"

"Information. Can a High Demon hide a fragment of their essence inside the host of another demon?"

He frowned, his forehead furrowing. I studied him, trying to decide if this response was an act. Or if perhaps Lilith was controlling him. And if so, was he even aware she was in there?

It would be just like Lilith to hide inside a demon who reviled her.

"You believe that Lilith has done this thing? Hidden her essence within one of my kind?"

"It's just a theory. But it's a strong one."

"I do not have the answer you seek."

I nodded slowly, then looked at the others, all of whom were watching me quizzically. All except Eric. We'd worked together for too long. He knew how I thought. "How about this, then? If we find her, will you fight with us?"

"It is one thing to provide you information regarding such an exalted High Demon. It is quite another to actively defy her."

"You understand, that if we're right—if she has hidden her essence in this realm—it means she is trying to become corporeal. You say she is looking for Solomon's Stone. It doesn't exist anymore, but if there is one ritual, there may be another. And if she completes that ritual, she will walk this earth, and you and your allies will be subjugated to her."

"I understood that you intended to stop her."

"That's the plan. But I never said we wouldn't need help. We need it. She really is trying to become corporeal. She's taken my daughter, and she intends to use a ritual to manifest inside Allie. She failed once. She is going to do her very best to not fail again."

Everything I was saying was true, and even as I spoke, panic rose inside me. *Allie.* All our thinking and searching, and we still weren't closer to saving her.

I lifted my chin, forcing myself to focus only on the moment. "Yes, I will fight her. But do you really want to stand there and let a human fight your battles?"

"Do not play mind games with a demon, Katherine Crowe."

I ignored his taunt with my former name. "No games. I mean what I say. We need help."

I took a step closer. "You once told me that you don't want to be subjugated to her. We both know that you would be if she is able to become both corporeal and fully empowered. There's never been a demon like that," I said. "A High Demon in the flesh without leaving a part of their demonic essence behind. She would rule on earth. We both know it."

"What you say is true. If Lilith is able to manage this thing, it will be different than anything we have seen before. And she will usher in a new age for my kind that I do not wish to see."

"So will you help?"

"I cannot. You should understand these things better, Hunter. I cannot go against Lilith."

"Is that because Lilith is inside you?"

He chuckled. "She is not."

"Are you sure?"

He blinked, and in that moment I saw his doubt. He believed that she could put her essence in a demon. And he worried that she might be in him. I was trained not to sympathize with demons, but in that moment, I felt genuinely sorry for him.

"Let's find out," I said, glancing over my shoulder at Eric.

He pulled the ruby from his pocket. He put it in is palm and held it out as in an offering.

"Touch it," he said.

Eliza looked between me and Eric. "What's going on?"

"Quiric knows."

"A ruby will turn black when touched by even the essence of she that came first." His brow furrowed. "This is not well-known among humans."

"We do our job well. Now touch it. Prove to us that she is not within you."

He reached for the ruby, then hesitated. "I confess..." he began and I held my breath, my body tense and ready for an attack. Around me, I saw Eric, Marcus, and Eliza shift, too, readying themselves for whatever came next.

"Confess what?" I asked.

He lifted his chin and met my eyes. "I confess that I am fearful."

I relaxed. Just slightly. "Why?"

"I do not believe that the she-beast is within me. But how can I be certain?" He looked to each of us. "How can any creature ever be certain of what is truly within them?"

"Very philosophical words coming from a demon."

"Perhaps you do not understand our kind as much as you think you do."

I glanced at Eric. "I understand you just fine. Touch the stone."

He hesitated, but then he reached out and took the ruby. He closed his hand around it. At the same time, Marcus edged Ren and Ana further back, and Eliza moved closer, her stiletto aimed right at his eye.

He opened his hand.

The stone was red.

I sagged with relief. And, I noticed, so did Quiric. I would never fully trust a demon, but he was right. There was no way to truly know what was inside anybody.

"I thank you, Katherine Crowe, for showing me my true nature."

"Don't think you're baiting me. We both know my name."

He said nothing, but I saw his smile. A kind of dark malevolence. And I knew that despite this reasonably civil conversation, he was truly still a demon.

"An offer," I said, with a glance toward Eric. "We need him."

He tilted his head. "It's risky," he said, confirming that he understood what I was thinking.

"Worth the risk?"

A moment passed, then he nodded. He turned to Quiric. "Lilith ordered one of her soldiers to take Allie. A boy."

"Ah. He has turned one of your students into one of her pets."

"He has," Eric said. "And we intend to get our daughter back. Help us rescue her. Lilith might be there, her essence hidden in one of the many demons who serve her, unlike you. Or she might not be there at all. We might be wrong, and none of Lilith's essence is this realm. Either way, help us, and the debt is paid."

"Debt?"

"The free pass you gave us for closing the gate," I said. "Gone. Poof. You help us, and you and your friends owe us nothing."

"Kate," Eliza said, but I shook my head. "It's Allie," I told her. "We have to. We're going up against Lilith. We need as big an army as we can gather."

She nodded. She looked terrified, but she nodded.

"Especially since we don't know what condition Allie will be in. If she's been drugged, she may have no strength to help in her own rescue." I returned my attention to Quiric. "If the gates open again, she is the only one who can close them. By helping her, you protect yourself."

A moment passed before he nodded. "Very well," Quiric said. "Eric Crowe, Katherine Crowe. We have a deal."

18

Now we had an army, but no field of engagement. At least, I hoped we had an army. To be honest, I didn't know whether or not I could trust Quiric and his fellow demons to keep their word. They were, after all, demons, and not known for their loyalty or respect of rules.

Still, they understood Allie's importance. If Allie died or Lilith took her body, their last hope of locking the remaining gates to Hell would be shattered. And since she was the last of Eric's genetic line, there would be no one else with that ability.

"You look like you're thinking serious thoughts," Laura said. We were at Cutter's worktable in the training room, both of us needing a break from living at the makeshift workstation we once called a dining table. "Do you have ideas on where we might find her?"

I shook my head. "No. I was wondering if Quiric and his crew will really show up if we go to battle.'"

"They will."

I smiled at my friend. "You have no way of knowing that."

"I'm an optimist. I'm not going to let this job change that." She smiled at me, and I knew she was trying to lighten the moment. But it didn't feel like anything could be light again. Not until I knew that my daughter was okay.

"How can I go on if I lose her?"

"You won't lose her," Laura said. "You have to believe that."

I nodded. "I know. I do. And I'm trying. But every hour that goes by makes it harder."

"She's still alive. She has to be. She's bait for Lilith's trap. You know it. I know it."

"Unless Lilith has already found Solomon's Stone."

"I thought you said it didn't exist."

"It doesn't. The stone was in the ring, and the ring was destroyed. Trust me, I remember."

"So why did Quiric say she was looking for Solomon's Stone?"

I stood and started pacing. "I don't know. It doesn't make sense."

I went to the freestanding heavy bag and got a few good kicks in. It felt good. Definitely better than sitting and thinking and not getting anywhere.

"Ana and Ren should be in here." I said.

"They're downstairs researching."

"I know, but they need to be training."

"All things in their time," Laura said. "They're doing the research that needs to be done."

I let go with another kick. "I know. I'm a mess. I'm sorry."

"I think you have reason to be."

"I was thinking about Allie earlier. About her children." I looked over at Laura, whose eyes were wide.

"Is there something you haven't told me?"

"I hope not," I said. "If there is, I'm going to have harsh words with Jared." We shared a smile and for a moment—one tiny little moment—everything felt lighter. Then the weight of everything pressed down again, and it felt like my back was going to break.

"Tell me," she said, getting up and tugging me over to a bench to sit. I managed it for about a second, then stood up and started to pace. But in deference to Laura, I stopped kicking things.

"I was thinking that she's the last of a line. If Lilith really does win and takes Allie out, then if one of those gates opens again they can't be closed. That would be the end. The real end."

"Yeah," Laura said. "I hadn't let myself think about that."

"And it's all on my family. Mine and Eric's. I don't know how to feel about that."

"About creating the gates? You don't have to feel anything at all. Not anything other than the rest of us do. Scared, angry, confused. But it's not your fault, Kate. You weren't around."

"True. But now Allie has the power to stop it. What if I can't protect her? What if she can't protect herself?"

"You're thinking that if Allie has kids, the line will continue. That she'll be the mother of the next generations of Demon Hunters with the power to close those gates."

"It sounds crazy when you say it, but it's true."

"There's always Eric."

"No, I told you. He tried to close the gate. We assumed he was the one. But it didn't work. It's Allie."

"And he's Allie's father."

"Oh." She's right. I'd never thought of that. If Eric had more children, they might be like Allie.

"Do you think it's all on him? Or is Allie what she is because of both of you?"

"I don't see what I could have brought to the mix."

"Yeah, but how could you? You don't know a thing about your parents. Not really."

I shook my head, not liking this whole conversation.

"You brought it up," Laura said, when I told her so.

"I don't want to think about Allie dying or Eric having more kids."

"I get that," she said, her eyes a little too understanding.

I turned away.

"Want to talk about it?"

"I hate it when you read my mind."

"No you don't. I can only do it because your my best friend. Ergo, you love me."

I laughed. "Now I really do hate you."

"Has it been going on for long?"

I sighed, giving in. "Just once. Right before Stuart woke up."

"Oh. Well, that's awkward."

"Thank you for that insight," I snapped, and we both laughed. For a second, it even felt good.

"Just tell me if you're okay."

"I'm fine. Or, no, I'm confused. And I'm feeling terribly guilty. But all of that is very petty compared to what I need to be doing."

"Have you told Stuart?"

"No. I need to, but no."

She frowned, then sat back, studying me. "Are you sure you need to? Are you doing it only to clear your conscience, or are you planning to leave him? Because if it's just to clear your conscience, and it's not going to happen again, then maybe you shouldn't say anything."

"Do you really believe that? Paul cheated."

"And if it had been once and I never knew about it?" She shrugged. "That would have been better, I think."

"Really?"

"I don't know. But it wasn't one time and he didn't cheat on me with a woman who was also the wife he lost only because he died."

She squeezed my hand. "You're in a completely different situation than every other person on this planet. Cut yourself a little slack, okay?"

"Why haven't they reached out?"

Her brow furrowed. "The other people on the planet?"

"No. Changing topics. Lilith's demony minions. When Lilith kidnapped Celia, arranged for Celia to reach out telepathically to Jared. It was just to torment him, but she did it. Why hasn't she done the same with Allie?"

"Maybe because you guys aren't telepathically connected?"

"Maybe. But it seems like she'd want to taunt me. I mean, right now I make a pretty good target. Highly emotional. Very tightly strung."

"She's being careful. Or maybe she has a weakness and doesn't want you to get a hint."

I stood up and started pacing again. "I like that. And if we can find and exploit it, we'll get Allie back."

"What do you think the weakness could be?"

"No idea. Or maybe Solomon's Stone. Quiric said she was looking for it. But she won't find it since it doesn't exist. That's not a weakness so much as—I don't know, but something not convenient for her. She needs it for the ritual. I'm guessing that in this new ritual she supposedly has, Solomon's Stone does the same thing as the chalice stone did before."

"Before, she wanted Eric, too."

I frowned. "Yeah. He's being careful. I can't lose both of them."

I glanced down at my wedding ring. "I have to tell him, " I whispered.

"I guess you do," Laura said. "For what it's worth, I think he'll understand."

I found Stuart in the bedroom, his back against the headboard. His eyes were closed and a book lay open on his lap.

I knew he was frustrated from being constantly interrupted, and I hated to wake him, but Laura was right. We needed to talk.

With a deep breath for courage, I stepped inside and shut the door, and when I looked back at him again, his eyes were open.

"Hey." He smiled, then patted the bed beside him. "Come tell me how it's going."

"Unfortunately, there's not a lot to tell," I said, sliding onto the bed beside him. I leaned close as he put his arm around me, then closed my eyes, relishing the familiar comfort.

He kissed the top of my head. "I'm sorry. I keep thinking that if I could force these visions to come, I could be more help. But I guess it doesn't work that way."

"Don't try, okay? You need to work on recovering."

"This might be more important. The message about the ruby meant something."

"It did. I think they all do, if we know how to interpret them. But you still need your rest."

He nodded, but clearly wasn't paying attention.

"Where do you think they come from?"

"You're asking the wrong person," I said. "That kind of question is more Eric's cup of tea."

The moment I said his name, I regretted it, because all it did was remind me of why I'd come here in the first place. I leaned in closer, not wanting to destroy this moment, and at the same time, knowing I had to.

I cleared my throat. "Listen, we need to talk."

"What's on your mind?"

I sat up, then shifted until I was sitting cross-legged on the bed so that I could see his face. I cleared my throat and tried to figure out how to begin. Since I had no clue, I just dove in. "So, right. It's just that—well, you know that I still love Eric."

He held up a hand. "I know where you're going with this."

"You do?" I was completely mortified.

"Yes. Of course. He and I had been trying to reach a détente. You'd seen the tension between us. It wasn't fair to anyone, least of all you."

"Um, right. I remember."

"I think we had—come to some sort of truce, I mean. I hope you could tell."

"Yes. I could. And I appreciate both of your efforts. It meant the world to me." I tell myself I should steer the conversation back around, but I'm severely lacking in motivation to do that. So I let him continue.

"But I screwed up even worse after we got back from Rome."

Now we weren't going in the direction I was expecting. "What are you talking about?"

"I'm talking about Allie. About what a shit I was to her after I learned about what she was. I treated her differently. Everyone was talking about there being a demon inside her that came from Eric. And I think I sabotaged whatever friendship I'd gained with him, and I know I acted horribly to her, my own daughter. Or, step-daughter, I mean."

I squeezed his hand. "Daughter works just fine," I said firmly. "And you're right. You were a mess. Standoff-ish. Scared. She noticed. So did I."

"Kate, I'm sorry."

I squeezed his hand. "You didn't let me finish. We noticed, yeah. But you came through in the end. Stuart, you sacrificed yourself for Allie. For Eric too, but I think that was just a secondary result."

At that, he laughed, and the moment felt lighter. Then the laugher faded.

"I don't know," he said. "I feel like that was too late to fix things with her."

"It wasn't. And even if you hadn't done that amazing thing—even if none of this had ever happened—we would still have gotten past it. Allie knows you love her. She was weirded out by learning about herself, too. So was I. I just can't show it as much. I'm her mom, and a Demon Hunter. I'm not supposed to let things like that wig me out."

"You're saying we're okay?"

"Of course, we are. And as soon as we get Allie back, you can tell her all of this, too."

He reached over and held my left hand, running his

thumb over the diamond of my wedding set. "I will. I love you, Kate."

"I love you, too, Stuart."

"I do." He stretched, then smiled. "So that's off my chest. Did you want to talk about something?"

I started to say that it could wait, but I got distracted by the way his thumb was moving on my ring, making the stone wink in the light. It was small, bought when Stuart was still working as an attorney for the County, and making very little money.

I kept watching, thinking. The little glimpses of white. The flashes of color. All from those little cuts in the stone.

It reminded me of crystals. And the way they grew. And that reminded me of Celia, trapped somewhere, probably locked in a crystal vault if she was even still alive.

Alone and scared.

Trapped.

Trapped in crystal. Trapped in stone.

I whipped my head up. "Stuart, I have to go down-stairs. I just realized something, and I need to go right now."

19

"I'm not finding anything," Eliza said the next morning, after we'd worked through the night, trying to chase down my theory. She slammed her laptop closed, then banged her head on the case. "Anybody else?"

Everyone at the table shook their heads. Eliza grimaced. "At least I'm not alone."

"We've got your back," Marcus said, reaching over to rub her shoulders. She tilted her head and smiled at him, then sighed as if in bliss.

I glanced down to hide my expression as I wondered what might be brewing there. From the way Ana and Ren were looking at each other and then over to Eliza, I assumed they were wondering the same thing.

I caught Ana's eye, then glanced down at my own computer as if in command. She swallowed, then her fingers started flying across the keyboard.

"I don't even know where else to look," Ren said.

"We've looked at all the auction houses. Maybe whole-salers in the diamond district?"

"That's not bad," Laura said. "And it's worth a shot. We're not getting anywhere."

Last night, I'd come to them to explain how looking at my ring had reminded me of cut crystals. And that had reminded me of Celia, trapped in a crystal vault.

And who else had been trapped? A demon, put in a cage cut from a gemstone. Trapped by Solomon himself.

"We know all of that," Ren had said.

"Yes, but do you know about all the extras?"

They'd looked at me like I was insane, all except Eric. He'd followed my lead down a very windy and weird path, finally learning that over seven centuries ago, some prince I'd never heard of in a country that no longer existed had traded something called the Remnant for a bride.

That was hardly earth shattering, but what fascinated Eric was a cross-reference about the Remnant. That article indicated that the full name of the Remnant was actually the Remnant of Ornias.

"What's the big deal about that?" Ana had asked.

"It's actually pretty cool," I'd said, as Eric had gawked at me. "What?" I'd asked. "I can't be interested in the historical stuff, too?"

"Just tell us," Ren had said, and Eric had waved a hand, urging me to proceed.

I did. After all, I knew this story well. The damn stone had wreaked quite a bit of havoc in my life, after all.

"Either of you know who Ornias is?"

They both shook their heads. "You, two?" I'd added, pulling Mindy and Jared into the makeshift class session.

"He was the demon that was bothering King Solomon while he was trying to build a temple," Mindy said.

"Right," Jared said. "I remember this story. He was such a pest that the king asked God for help and was rewarded with a stone imbued with the power to trap demons."

"So he trapped Ornias?" Ren asked.

"Yup," I'd said.

"But he wanted to torment the demon," Jared continued. "So he had the stone cut smaller and smaller, making Ornias more and more uncomfortable in his gemstone prison."

"Then the king had the stone set into a ring," Mindy concluded.

Ana frowned. "What ?" I'd asked her.

"So that means that the Remnant of Ornias is the part King Solomon had cut away?"

"Bingo." That from Eric. "In this kind of research— chasing demons, I mean—that's one hell of a clue. Can you tell me why?"

Ana and Ren had looked at each other. "Because it proves the pieces of the stone we're looking for really did exist."

"Exactly. Although it's not exactly proof. Let's call it strong evidence. And it gives us a place to go next."

"Which is?" Jared had asked. To which Eric had

sighed and gone back to the computer to try and catch another glimpse of our elusive Remnant.

Unfortunately, that had been the only real breakthrough for hours, and now we were all getting tired and loopy. I was about to pack it all in and grab a catnap when Marcus whistled. "Check this announcement: Set of cut gemstones said to have mystical powers and once used for purchase of royal bride sold at auction to anonymous buyer."

"Sold by who?" Mindy asked. "And who's the anonymous buyer?"

We all stared at her until she rolled her eyes. "Yes, I know what anonymous means. I'm just really tired."

"And there's no mention of the seller, either. This is a compilation document."

"Does it have a date?" I waited as Marcus searched the document.

He shook his head. "No. Just a general compilation. Can't tell how old it is.

"Could be Lilith," Jared said. "We have to assume she has Solomon's Stone now. And her essence is inside one of her minions. And she has Allie."

"Everything she needs," I said, "and we still don't have a clue where to find her."

"The buyer might not be Lilith."

I ignored Eric. "For all we know she's already performed the ritual and Allie is—"

I pushed back from the table, unable to even deal with the thought. "I'm sorry. I just need some space right now."

I turned to leave, and found Stuart standing in the doorway to the dining room wearing nothing but his pajama bottoms.

"Stuart? Are you okay?"

He blinked, and I hurried toward him, but he stepped back, his hands up as if to ward me off.

"Stuart?"

He looked around the room, his eyes falling on Jared before they rolled back into his head. He spread his arms, then began to speak.

"She lives. Deep inside. Hidden in the hills. Battled in the dark light that burns no more. From many to none. Abandoned, yet full."

I heard an odd clicking, and realized that someone was typing, taking down his words. I only had a moment to register that thought when his body went as limp as spaghetti, and he collapsed in a heap on the ground.

Ren stared at his screen as if he was staring at a ghost.

"I know this," he said. "I know this, but I just can't remember."

I looked up from where I was kneeling by Stuart. "Somebody, help me get him to the couch." Marcus hurried over and together we helped a half-conscious Stuart walk that direction. As we moved, I glanced over at Ren. "What are you talking about? How is it familiar?"

"What Stuart just said." The frustration was clear in his voice. "It reminds me of something. And I feel like I should know this, but I can't get it in my head."

"Well, let's just take it line-by-line then," Ana said. "She lives. Who?"

"Lilith," Jared said. His voice flat. "That has to be it, right? All of our worrying about how we were going to get Allie back, and it's all over. Lilith is inside her now. She's stolen Allie from me, and my sister, too."

"No," I said, from where I'd slid to the floor beside Stuart's sofa. "No, I'm not going to believe it, and neither are you. We don't know that. I don't believe it."

"I don't either," Eric said. "I turned to see him standing in the doorway.

"You heard?"

"I heard," he said, then crossed to me and pulled me up. I collapsed into his arms, then felt Stuart's hand gently touch my leg. I cringed, lost and confused as I took comfort from these two men.

"I don't believe it," Eric repeated. "If it were true, Lilith would have contacted us somehow. We'd know. We'd know, because she'd want to rub it in our faces. To show herself to us first. Lilith in Allie's body."

He shuddered. "No," he said. It's not true. It's what she wants, but it's not true."

"He's right," Stuart said, his voice throaty but discernible.

I turned around, something in his tone tugging at me. "Do you know that? Like in a vision?"

"Not sure. Think so. She feels ... alive. More than ... wishful thinking."

I closed my eyes and prayed. Then rolled my shoulders back, told myself to get it together, and got back to work. Because right then, those were the only things I could do.

"It might not be Lilith at all," Eliza said. "Stuart might actually have been referring to Jared's sister. Maybe she's the one who's still alive."

"You could be right," I said as I pulled a blanket over Stuart, whose eyes were fluttering shut. "It could be Celia. For that matter, it could be Allie," I added, because I liked that option better than the alternative.

"Stuart's vision or prophecy or whatever you call it could be telling us that there's still time to stop whatever it is that Lilith's up to."

"There's just no way to be certain," Laura said.

"I know. All we can do is keep looking and hoping that we're not too late." I sounded so calm, but I didn't feel calm. I felt frantic. We had too many possibilities and too few answers.

I knelt beside Stuart and took his hand. "Hey," I said softly. "You remembered what you said."

"Barely." The word is soft, almost inaudible. "Feelings, not words."

"Do you remember anything else? Any more feelings?"

"No. Nothing. So tired. Sorry."

"It's fine," I said, even as I mentally cursed. Then I stood up. "Okay, here's what we're going to do. Write what he said on a white board and that way we can refer to it. Maybe it will seem familiar to someone else."

"We don't have a whiteboard," Mindy said.

"Then write it on the walls in a Sharpie," I snapped. "We can paint the damn wall later once we buy a stupid whiteboard."

"Right. Okay. On it." Mindy sprang to her feet and ran to find a Sharpie. Then, as the others looked on, she started to write Stuart's cryptic words on the wall in crisp handwriting as Ana recited it back to her.

"Anything sound familiar?" I asked. "Anybody? Ren? Have you figured it out yet?"

"No. Sorry."

"Me neither," Ana said. "Except..."

"What?"

"Nothing specific in the actual words, but it still feels like something I've seen or heard."

"Seen? Okay, try to dial that in," I told her.

"I told you, there's something familiar about this," Ren said.

I looked at all of them. "Then figure out what it is."

"Okay," Ren said. "One step at a time. This second part. Deep inside. Hidden in the hills. That must mean something inside a mountain. A cave probably. Or some sort of building that's built into a hillside. Didn't one of Jared's telepathic communications with Celia say something about the house being buried?"

Jared, who'd been pacing, stopped. "You're right. That's good. Nearby. Some sort of construction built into a hill." He looked around the table, then pointed to Marcus. "You're decent on a computer, right?"

"Reasonably," Marcus said. "Mostly I'm a trainer, the research side isn't usually my thing."

"It doesn't matter. Start trying to find any sort of architectural plans or permits for buildings built into the hills on the east side of San Diablo."

"Right. I'll do my best," Marcus said.

"I'm on it too," Eric said from the doorway. "At least until somebody calls me back about the damn Remnant." I knew that he'd started the day with dozens of calls, trying to find the chain of title for the remnant stones. "I tried everybody I could think of. I've got people all over the world working on it. But no luck so far."

"Well, this is a totally different puzzle to tackle," I said.

He frowned. "Battled in the dark light that burns no more." He shook his head. "Not ringing any bells at all."

"Daddy!" I turned around to see Timmy running towards Stuart, who was out cold now. Timmy scrambled up, curled up on his dad, stuck his thumb in his mouth, and closed his eyes, too. I sighed, desperately wishing I could set aside this day that easily.

In the doorway, Fran offered an apologetic smile. "I'm so sorry. I know you all have a crisis on your hands. But he really wanted to see his daddy."

"It's okay," I told her. "I think they're fine for now."

"Well, good. Can I help? I could ask Signora Micari to bring you some snacks."

"That would be very nice, actually," Eric said.

Fran pointed across the room. "I can cut to the kitchen through there, right?"

"Absolutely," I said. But she didn't seem to have heard me. Instead she was staring at the wall. Mindy had finished transcribing the words from Stuart's trance, and Fran walked closer to them.

"Battled in the dark light that burns no more," she read aloud. She turned to face me, then Eric. "What is this?"

"Stuart's started having visions or trance-speech or something. He doesn't know what it means, and we're trying to figure it out."

"It sounds really familiar," Ren said for the millionth time.

"To me, too," Fran said. "It was in a book I had when I was a little girl."

"What? Seriously?" I hurried to her side, as did Eric. Everyone else just stared at her. "What book?"

"Years and years ago," she said. "I had a book of scary local stories and supernatural things. Supposedly true. Got it from some used bookstore. I was probably ten, maybe eleven, but the book was for adults."

"Do you still have it?"

She shook her head. "I don't even remember what it was called. Or the story, honestly. Not in detail, anyway. All I recall is that there was a dark tribe centuries ago. Not satanic worshipers. No, the book said they invited in the demons."

She looked at me, her eyes wide, and I nodded for her to go on.

"I remember thinking that was so creepy when I was a little girl. They were like a cult, if that's what you called it back then."

"That's it," Ren said. "That's what I've been trying to remember. They were called something like the Bringers of the Dark Light, only not in English, obviously. And eventually they fought with the missionaries."

"Go on," Eric urged.

Ren bit his lip, obviously trying to remember. "Most people called it folklore because it never ended up in textbooks, but I read about it when I was a kid. I used to read all sorts of stuff about the Aztecs and Mayans. All those civilizations."

"The part about From many to None, Abandoned yet Full makes sense too," Fran said. "At one point, it was supposed to have been a thriving community. Then they died out."

"Might have been a city of demons," Laura suggested. "Then early hunters found them. Or is that stupid?"

"Not stupid at all," I said. *Forza* actually existed back then, and its Hunters traveled all over the globe. Even to places the Vatican won't acknowledge now."

"Now, they say it's haunted by the ghosts of those past worshipers," Ren said.

"A place for incorporeal demons to interact with those who are embodied," I suggested. "This is all promising. It's out of the way, clearly had space, and

230

most likely had cells for those who stumbled upon them."

"So how do we find it," Jared asked.

"Good question," Eric said. "If it's as old as that, it's certainly not going to be in architectural records. Ren, since you seem to remember those details, do you think that you could look at some old maps of the mission trails around San Diablo? It's likely the missionaries set up camp close by the demons, hoping to convert them."

"On it," Ren said. "Someone else should search, too, though. We'll race to the answer."

"Done," Ana and Laura said in unison.

"So if we're lucky, we'll know her location soon," I said. "But we still don't know about the Remnant. Eric's waiting for calls. How about Quiric?" I asked Jared. "Were you able to find him?"

"Yeah, I tracked his scent. He says he doesn't know anything. But he also says that he'll keep his promise and help us when and if we need him and his merry band of demons."

He started to pace. "I need to go back out there," he said. "I need to be doing something. The two women I love are out there, and we don't have a clue where to go."

"Trust me," Eric said. "I know how you feel. But there's nowhere to go until we know our destination."

"It could take these guys days to find this place," he said, his hand indicated Ren and the others. "In the meantime, we can't just—"

He froze.

His body just went completely stiff and then, very

slowly, he put his hands to his forehead and squeezed his eyes closed.

"Jared?" I hurried toward his side, suddenly terrified. "Jared, are you okay?"

For a moment nothing changed, then he gasped and opened his eyes. They were glassy, and he shook his head as if trying to remember where he was.

Then he said one word: "Celia."

I moved closer. "What?"

"It was her. She was calling out to me."

"Telepathically...?"

"Yes, *yes*. She must have somehow gotten free." He'd lost the tone of shock and was all business, crisp and efficient. "She showed me a symbol. Showed me some landmarks she remembered from when they first took her. And she asked me to hurry. Begged me. She said they're planning something, and then she screamed, and then the vision went away."

"A symbol?"

Jared grabbed the Sharpie and went to the wall, then started to scribble until the wall displayed a circle filled with crisscrossing lines intersecting another circle.

"That's perfect," Ren said. "Just let me..." He trailed off as his fingers flew over the computer. "Okay, yeah, that symbol ties with a tribe that was established around here," he said, pointing to the map on his screen. The area was in the hills above San Diablo, about a mile away from a public campground.

"That's close," Ren said. "Jared, once we're there, do

you think you can track them? Any demon scent heading into the woods would be them, right?"

"Good thinking," Jared said. "I yeah. I can totally track them."

It took three more hours, and four more telepathic messages between Jared and Celia, but we were finally on our way. Apparently Jared's sister had been able to escape from her crystal vault, when one of Lilith's minions had failed to secure it properly.

"She's fine," the girl had told Jared when he'd asked about Allie. "She talks to me. She helped me. We've helped each other."

"Thankfully she seems to have come through her ordeal intact," Jared said to me, after he relayed one of their conversations. "She sounds sane. Nothing like what she was before. I think they left her alone. I think that gave her time to heal. And I think having Allie with her helped her find the way back."

I reached for his hand. "I'm so glad to hear it."

A team of us were in the van, and between Celia's information and Ren's research, we were able to locate the probable location of the walking path from the public camping at the demonic cult's ancient homestead in the wilderness.

Celia promised to keep guiding us, and I could only hope that would work. We still didn't know where the

Remnant was. And if Lilith already had it, she could be performing the ritual right now.

Celia seemed to think that wasn't the case. She told Jared that the demons who served Lilith had been coming and going, and she'd heard them talking about a search and a gemstone. I only hoped that meant that we still had time to find it first and ruin any chance she had of getting inside of Allie.

Because there was a chance. Eddie had tracked down the actual ritual, and we now knew that it was essentially the same as before. Lilith would use the Remnant in lieu of the chalice stone. Her essence would flow from the host to the Remnant and into the vessel, presumably Allie.

Before, she'd needed Eric's blood as well. There was no mention of that in the ritual we found, though it did mention a catalyst. And since none of Lilith's minions had made a play to capture Eric, I feared the catalyst was something a lot easier to come by.

Our only real chance was to find and destroy the Remnant. Do that, and Lilith's bit of essence could either zip back off into the ether or just hang around waiting for the body to slowly decay.

In the passenger seat, I pulled my feet up and hugged my knees to my chest. This was the worst part. The waiting. I wanted to be in the fight. I wanted to be battling for my little girl. I didn't want to be driving to a park like we were going camping.

I hated camping.

We turned off the main road to a gravel road, then

turned onto a dirt road that was still technically in the park, but well away from the campsites.

We got out, then started searching for the trail we knew had to be close by.

"Are we sure this is the right direction?" I asked.

"If what Ren read from the maps that he found—and if what Celia remembered and told Jared—is correct, we should be," Cutter said.

"There" Eliza said. I turned around and saw her pointing slightly east. "That tree. Didn't Celia say something about a dead tree with blackened bark marking the path?"

"She did," Jared said.

He'd asked her to relay anything that she remembered from the time that she was brought to this prison.

She'd been frantic and scared, but they hadn't blindfolded her. And while she didn't have many memories that would help without context, now that we were on sight, the few things she remembered made some sense.

That black tree.

A boulder that stuck into the path.

A small ancient graveyard that we passed as we descended a hill.

"We must be close," Cutter said. Laura had wanted to come, too, but we had all insisted that she stay behind. Eddie as well. He'd grumbled about it, and I did feel a little guilty. He might be in his eighties, but he was still spry.

Still, I needed him back at the school. We were sending our best fighters to rescue Allie and Celia. As far as I was concerned, we had no choice—too much was riding on getting Allie away from Lilith.

But I couldn't discount the possibility that this was a trap. So Laura, Marcus, Eddie, and Ana had stayed behind to protect the school, and Father Donnelly had come to join them, along with Doctor Carlton, who he'd asked to come, too, in case any of us came home injured.

Despite being a student, Ren was with us not because of his fighting—unfortunately, that was still mostly untested—but because of his familiarity with the stories about the cult. I hoped that there would be absolutely nothing for them to do. But I was certain, that if we hadn't protected the school, something horrible would've happened. And I couldn't bear the thought of losing Stuart and Timmy too.

"There" Eliza said, pointing to something in front of us.

At first I couldn't see what it was. Then the native camouflage seemed to fade, letting me see the lines of a structure built against the cliff wall. It was quite a piece of architecture.

As we cautiously approached, staying low and hoping we were going unnoticed, I realized how large the structure was. I hoped that the exterior didn't represent the size of the interior, because once we were inside, we could find ourselves in a cave-like maze of twisting corridors.

Celia had been very little help describing the interior since she only saw her small vault and the almost equally small room in which it existed.

And then, as if to eradicate any doubt we might have had that we were in the right place, a half dozen demons leaped from the trees above us, sending us tumbling to the ground and trying to get enough purchase to stand and take them out.

How did I know they were demons? Because they politely called us Hunters and told us to die.

That, and their breath, which I noticed when one leaped on me as I was flat on my back, his face close to mine. I thrust my head up to ram him in the forehead, rolling over as I did so. Then I pulled the clip out of my hair—worn for just this purpose—and rammed it through his eye.

"Damn it," Jared said, stabbing his demon through the eye with a nearby branch, "I should have had my knife ready."

"Yes," I said, kicking the body of the demon that had attacked me out of the way. "You damn sure should have."

He gave me a sideways look. "It won't happen again."

"I guess that was the welcoming party," I said looking around to see that everyone had handled the surprise invasion quite handily. A half dozen demon carcasses littered the ground around us, and we had suffered no serious injuries.

"Should we dare to think this is a good sign?" I asked.

Eric shot me a stern glance. "You should know better than to tempt fate. Come on."

It was surprisingly easy to find the front door, and even easier to enter.

"It's got to be a trap," Eliza said.

Jared mentally reached out again for Celia but there was nothing. "I can't even feel her," he said, his voice tight with worry. "What if they bugged out?"

"No. They're here," I said. I had no proof whatsoever that was true, but I couldn't stand the thought of any other answer.

Eric eyed me sideways, but I shook my head. "No. I don't want to hear it."

He gave a curt nod, and we continued on.

Once again, demons attacked as we entered the cave-like structure, and once again, we defeated them easily. My guess was that they were the away team, meant only to guard Celia, about whom Lilith didn't really care.

Meanwhile, she and her demonic minions—including the one with her essence—were taking Allie to some ritual site to perform the ceremony.

And the thought had me totally freaking out.

"We need to hurry," I said, running through my theory. Eric scowled, clearly agreeing with me.

"Go," Jared said. "I'll get Celia. Just go."

"No," Eric said. "We don't know where Lilith is taking her. We'll help you, we'll all go back, and we'll figure this out."

"She has the tracker," I said, referring to a necklace that had a small tracking device. We hadn't been able to see it before—I'd assumed that was because Bruce had stripped her jewelry. But maybe it was because of this freaky cave. Maybe as soon as we were out of here, we could track her.

A mother could hope.

Ten minutes later, this mother was starting to lose that hope. We were going in circles, Jared had no contact with Celia, and he could find a scent for her or Allie.

"Keep trying," I said.

"What do you think I'm—*wait*. Blood." He looked at me and my heart flipped. "Allie's blood."

I reached for Eric, and he squeezed my hand. "Remember," he said. "We don't worry until there's something to worry about," he said.

I repeated that to myself as we went deeper and deeper into the bowels of the cave until we finally ended up in a dark chamber, filled with rocks and shadows. Even shining my flashlight around, I saw nothing else. Not until Jared, with his preternatural vision, pointed toward a dark corner on the far side of the room where two forms huddled unmoving together.

"*No,*" I cried, racing that way with Eric right by my side.

I threw myself down, expecting the worse, then whimpered in relief when Allie murmured, "Mommy?"

"Baby," I cried, pulling her into my arms. She clung to me, then held out one arm for her dad, who also pulled her close.

Behind us, Jared was with his sister. I could hear his soft, consoling words. Then his louder, more tentative, "Allie?"

"I'm here," she said. "I'm okay."

"Really?" I asked, looking her over.

She nodded. "Yeah. She didn't hurt me. I think they

JULIE KENNER

were trying to hide us down here. I cut my thumb. I was hoping Jared could follow the blood."

"Smart girl," Eric said, and she smiled.

"And Celia? Celia, are you okay?"

"I'm okay. Thank you. Thank you for everything."

"I didn't do anything. You're the one who called to Jared."

"You talked to me. You got me out of my head. I think I was going a little crazy," Celia said. "Jared, I missed you."

"I missed you, too," he said, then hugged her from where they were crouched on the ground.

They stood when we did, and for a moment, Allie seemed frozen. Then she threw herself into his arms and kissed him.

Eric shoved his hands into his pockets.

I tried to hide a smile.

And Jared gently pushed her away. "Your parents."

"Do you really care?"

He glanced my way, then shrugged. "Actually, I don't," he said. And then he kissed her back.

J ared, Allie, and Celia claimed the back seat of the van as we all headed back to the academy. Eric was driving, and I caught him checking his rearview mirror far more often than was truly necessary considering there was barely any traffic.

I shot him a few amused, sideways glances, but didn't say anything. To be honest, I might have pulled down my visor a few times and taken some peeks myself. Celia's head rested against her brother's arm, and her eyes were closed. Poor thing was probably exhausted. Allie leaned in from the other side, and his arm was curled around her. Twice I saw him brush his lips over her hair, and her soft, answering smile.

Honestly, they made a good couple. He was too old for her, that's for sure. But considering the world we lived in, maybe that didn't matter. He'd protect her and he'd help her and he'dlove her, I was sure of that. And when your life evolves around hunting demons, there wasn't much more important than that.

The others sat in the middle two rows, and the chatter on the drive back was as expected. I only half listened. The bottom line was that we still needed to figure out where Lilith's essence was hiding. And that was important. But right then, all I wanted to do was revel in the fact that we rescued these two young women. Celia, who looked positively giddy that her brother was kissing Allie, and Allie herself, not just because the world couldn't afford to lose her, but because Eric and I certainly couldn't.

"I think we've bought some time," Cutter said, pulling me away from my rambling thoughts.

"What makes you think that?"

"Lilith's in retreat. She wouldn't have left Allie behind if she was ready for the ritual. She must be missing some important piece. I'm guessing the Remnant."

"I was thinking the same thing," Eric said.

"Even so, why let Allie go?" I asked, lowering my voice. It wasn't a secret, but Allie and Celia had already been through so much.

"Probably because she knows that if she keeps Allie with her, you two will never rest," Eliza chimed in. "You'll be hounding her, searching for her. And you're good. You'd probably find her."

I looked back at Eliza, who shrugged. "Just telling it like it is. This way, she buys herself some time with out you constantly riding her back."

"It's a good theory," Cutter said.

"Yeah," Ren said. "It makes sense to me."

"The downside is that she runs the risk of something happening to Allie," Eric said. "But under the circumstances you're probably right. But Allie," he said, raising his voice to catch her attention, "you're going to have to stay vigilant."

From the very back seat, Allie said, "What? Were you talking to me?"

Everyone in the van began laughing as Allie looked around, bewildered. Then she shrugged, shot me a grin and snuggled back into Jared's arms.

I bit back a smile as I turned in my seat to face forward, trying hard not to look at Eric.

"We are so going to have a talk," he murmured.

I was distracted from thinking about other ways to torment him with the fact that his daughter was growing up when his phone chirped with an incoming text. "Want me to check that?"

"Sure. Read it to me."

I opened his phone and found the text message at the top of the list. "I don't know who it's from. Just a number and I don't recognize the area code. But it says, *Record found. Sale 27 yrs ago to TM, as u suspected.*

I shifted in my seat to face. "What does that mean?"

"It means that Theophilus Monroe purchased the Remnant. And since we've found no other transaction, it's a good bet he kept the stones."

"Right up his alley," I said. "That's for sure."

Eliza leaned forward, apparently having overheard the conversation. "Was he living in the mansion then?"

"I believe so," Eric said. "If not, he had access. It was owned by his family or extended family for generations."

"You think the Remnant's in the mansion," Eliza said. "Theo, you crazy old bastard."

I choked out a laugh.

"Are you surprised?" Eric asked. "The man collected every supernatural item he could find."

"Okay, but where?" Eliza asked. "The place has been remodeled a zillion times over."

Eric didn't answer. Instead, he pressed the accelerator. I held tight to the armrest as we raced through traffic, the van not going nearly as fast as I wanted it to.

"It's probably nothing," I said aloud, hoping to calm my nerves. "We have no way of knowing if Lilith has this information too. I mean we've been searching forever."

"She's probably been searching forever too."

"If she thought she could get her hands on the Remnant, she wouldn't have left Allie behind. She needs Allie most of all."

He let up on the gas. "That's a good point."

"Well, yeah, but don't slow down. I mean, I could be wrong."

He increased our speed, but not so fast we would break the sound barrier. "We need to take more care vetting the staff," he said. "If she learns that Monroe possessed it, she'll try to find it on the property, and that means getting inside. She'll send whatever minion is housing the piece of her essence in as part of a delivery team or a new addition to housekeeping. All new staff holds the ruby. Deal?"

"Are you kidding? Of course." I frowned. "We need to find the Remnant and destroy it," I said. "Where do you think it is?"

"No idea. Considering that mansion, it could be anywhere. There could be wall safes we've never even seen. If Lilith's determined enough, she could summon an army of demon minions to tear apart the academy."

"Too bad she couldn't have done it before we did the remodel." He shot me a dark look. "Sorry. Gallows humor."

Ten minutes later we'd pulled the van into the garage, then entered through the kitchen. Doctor Carlton was there, looking flustered. "We were beginning to worry," he said. "Sit. I need to check your injuries."

"We're fine," I said, glancing at the zigzag of scrapes and cuts that covered all of our hands, arms, and faces.

"You were in the woods and then a cave where bacteria and parasites thrive. Now sit down and let me clean these."

We gave in—easier than arguing—and he took care of Jared's wounds, then ushered over Celia. "Such a pleasure to meet you," he said to the girl as he checked her over. "We are so delighted that you are out of danger."

"Thank you. I'm very pleased, too. May Jared and I go through? And Allie, please?" She held out her hand for Allie, who joined them with a smile.

While the doctor bandaged Allie's thumb, Celia came over and gave me a hug. "I truly thought I was losing my mind in the room where they held me, but these last few days with Allie have helped so much. I feel grounded again. As if there's really a future for me."

Her speech was poised and eloquent and I had to remind myself she was much older than ten. "I guess I'm trying to say that I feel optimistic about the future. So thank you—the two of you, she added to Eric—for the gift of your daughter."

We thanked her and gave her a hug, then she skipped back to join Allie and Jared as they moved through to the dining area.

"The rest of you are a mess," the doctor said. "Lean against the counter, all of you, and let me fix you up."

"This really isn't necessary," Eric said as the doctor moved down us like an assembly line with his package of antiseptic wipes and bandages. Legs one way, arms on the return, facial cuts on the next pass.

"No," the doctor said. "You're right. It's not. Your scrapes do need tending, but it's not urgent. The truth is the others are putting together a bit of a surprise for you. A celebration that Celia has been returned to the fold."

"Ah," Eliza said, as if a huge puzzle was falling into place. It was, actually. The whole triage in the kitchen thing really had been a bit odd.

"Promise me you'll act surprised. I wasn't supposed to say a thing."

We all agreed, of course, then moved through to the dining area and on to the entryway. I stumbled, feeling lightheaded, and Eric caught my arm.

I shook myself. It had been quite a morning.

But with the next step, I felt lighter still. Then dizzy. And then, suddenly, the room was spinning. Doctor Carlton took my arm and let me across the room. I tried to look for Eric, but the room was turning flips.

"Forgive me," the doctor said. "They have taken my daughter."

The words made no sense. They seemed to be spinning with my head. Nothing made sense. Not the words, not this room.

The entry hall was full of chairs, and all of our staff, students, and instructors were sitting down, their feet flat on the floor. Other people I'd never seen before mingled about, chatting as if they were at a party.

Was this supposed to be a party?

I looked up and saw Celia sitting on a chair as well. This one was facing the room, and she was tapping her feet.

Jared was there, too, pacing in front of her, his face contorted. Or was it my vision?

Beside me, Eric looked like he was having trouble keeping his head on. And I didn't see Allie anywhere.

"Alleeee?" I managed, but I'm not even sure Eric heard the word.

It didn't matter, I saw her next. Doctor Carlton carried her in with Bruce. She wore a thin white nightgown, and they put her on the ground in front of me and Eric. Then they lifted our feet, and pushed her closer so that when they put our feet back down, they were on her body.

I felt her heartbeat and wanted to weep with relief.

I tried to lift my feet, but they were stuck fast.

Then Bruce leaned into my face, his own spinning in front of me. Then, quickly and dispassionately, he sliced my legs with a razor. Slowly, blood began to trickle, reaching all the way to Allie's nightgown.

He did the same to Eric, then moved to stand in front of Jared. "It is done," Bruce said, then bowed.

That's when I realized.

Lilith.

She was in Jared.

Jared who was the only one in the room walking around. Jared, who had the tiniest, tiniest pinprick of demon inside of him from that ancestral demon from so long ago.

Jared, the man who had said that he loved my daughter and was now hosting Lilith. Had he taken her in intentionally? Or had she forced her way in? If the latter, he would never forgive himself. If the former, I would kill him myself. That is, assuming that I survived.

Then Celia stood, and once again my thoughts flipped. *Lilith*?

"Let the ritual begin," she said. "Let the queen who is within me be born into form. Let the catalyst bathe her body, and let the Remnant bind the witnesses and provide safe passage." She held up her hands, her eyes closed.

Frantic, I turned to Eric, my movements slow because of the drugs. *The wipes*, I realized. Transdermal drugs.

"How?" I whispered to Eric. "The Remnant?"

"I don't know." He was more clear now, too. The drug was wearing off. Hopefully, it was wearing off Allie even faster.

"No one is tied down. But no one is moving. I can't. Can you?"

"No. Mortar."

At first I thought he meant that his feet felt like they were in mortar, then I realized he meant the Remnant.

The stones had been crushed into the mortar.

Solomon's Stone had been created to trap a demon. Somehow, the Remnant had been altered simply to *trap.* And we all were, just like a bunny in a snare.

I glanced again at Jared, who was still pacing, his face contorted. His arms were moving jerkily at his side, the movement opposite to his legs. I shifted my gaze to Celia —Lilith—but she wasn't watching him.

"Feet off," Eric said, and I saw him slowly inch his feet backward. If we were the catalyst and we weren't touching Allie, maybe the spell wouldn't work.

I struggled, but managed to move my feet just the tiniest bit. Then Bruce and a demon came over. "I don't think so," Bruce said, then plunked my feet right back where they'd been.

"It is time," said Celia-Lilith in Celia's voice. "Lilith resides within me and without. She shall be made corporeal in this Vessel, subjugating the pitiful creature that inhabits this shell. But only part of my great being can exist in this form. And so the power and path of the Remnant and the blood of the catalysts shall render me flesh in a body with the strength to house my full essence, which I shall call to fill me.

"But I am not without pity to the one who will be trapped within. I shall give her a mate. Come, brother. Come and kneel before your sister-queen."

Jared's legs moved in jerky spasms, and I realized he was fighting the pull of Lilith's will, not the Remnant. He was in the area in the entry hall that didn't have the mystical mortar. And as for Lilith's power, as both a High Demon and one of the oldest demons, she had powers beyond what most demons did, even though she was only partially in Celia's body.

"Celia," he said. "Celia, I love you. Help me fight her. I only just got you back."

"Fool," hissed Lilith.

I watched the tears fill Jared's eyes. Of course he would never side with Lilith. I knew him better than that, didn't I? How could I have even thought it?

My only excuse was that I'd been drugged and confused. But the drugs were wearing off. And I was starting to see clearly again.

"You are mine," Lilith said. "Come bow before me."

It was clear he had no choice. He went. He fell to his knees.

"I will never bow to you. And I will never love you, no matter whose body you steal."

"Never love me?" The voice was Celia's. She blinked at him. "But I thought you would always love me. Always protect me."

The tears streamed freely down his face, and he

scooted closer. I held my breath, terrified he would fall for this ploy. The poor guy was already so broken.

"Kate," Eric said. "Feet."

I realized what he meant. I still couldn't stand, but I could inch my feet backward even more. Letting a hint of Celia come out had taken a toll on her power.

Slowly, Eric and I pulled our feet off Allie, stopping the trickle of blood. I held my breath, hoping no one would notice this time. I didn't think they would. Everyone was rapt on the scene between Celia-Lilith and Jared.

"I need you," she said in that sweet, childish voice. "You know it's true. I need you and I love you."

"I love you, too. Is it really you or is this a trick?"

"It's me. She pushes me down like in the vault. But I'm here. Don't make me be lonely for ever and ever. Stay with us."

He dropped to his knees and held out his arms, openly sobbing now. "Come here, baby sister."

I held my breath wanting to scream out to him but terrified what punishment might be rendered. Not to me, but to those I loved.

I finally saw Timmy, sitting far to the right in Fran's lap, her arms tight around him. His thumb was in his mouth and his eyes were wet and red. *I love you*, I mouthed and hoped he saw me and understood.

Even as I said those words, Jared said the same to his sister. Then he pushed her back gently, as if memorizing that sweet face.

"I'm sorry," he said at the same time that his hand

smashed forward, crashing through her ribcage, then ripping out her heart.

It was over.

The ceremony ended. Our bodies free to move.

On the ground, Allie sat up, her head shaking with confusion. "What happened?"

"Kill the host, the partial goes back to the source demon," I said, remembering what Eddie and told me.

"Huh?"

"I'll explain later. Jared's going to need you. Celia is dead. Lilith killed her."

"Oh." Her chin shook, but she didn't cry. Instead she nodded. "I'm there for him, but tell me what happened later." I promised I would, and she turned to find him.

As she did, a great howl filled the room, followed by a wild wind that almost blew me back in my chair.

I glanced at Eric, who said only one word. *Lilith*
Well, damn.

He was right, though. I was certain of it. Not only did it make sense, but the reanimated Celia corpse was a huge clue.

Demons *can* move into a dead body with organs missing, but they don't like to. Lilith definitely was beyond caring. She was *pissed*.

"Go for the limbs," I shouted as Allie, Eric, Jared and me rushed toward Celia's body, now animated by a pissed off High Demon.

Fortunately, she couldn't put her full essence in, or we'd really be screwed. As it was, the battle was a monster. She was still a High Demon, which meant her strength was beyond mine. And she was using almost all of it, the body already heating up. She didn't care. This was about destruction.

I had no weapon—Doctor Carlton must have taken my stiletto, but I picked up my chair, intending to use that.

Turns out I didn't need to. Allie was pissed off, too.

I watched as my daughter spun and kicked and leaped and jumped, ripping and tearing through arms and legs with such fury that I wondered if she would be able to shut it down. As it was, no one else could even get close to Lilith.

Finally, Lilith was nothing more than a pile of torn flesh, the demon gone, returned to the ether. Not killed in her true form, but gone for now at least.

I started to go to Allie, but Jared looked at me, a plea in his eyes. I nodded, and he knelt down beside her, holding her.

"I'm sorry," she said. "It wasn't Celia. It wasn't Celia I ripped apart."

"I know," he said, then whispered soft words as I turned away to let them grieve together.

And so I could get busy with the demon riot going on in our elegant entry hall. Because all the demons Lilith had invited to her little coming out celebration were still here, and they were looking for a brawl. And all of my students and staff felt pretty much the same. I looked around and saw Fran and Stuart slipping out the back with Timmy, Eddie accompanying them as their escort. I made a mental note to thank Eddie later. Right now, I had other things to do.

"She made a huge mess out of our fabulous new school," I said to Eric.

"That she did."

"Feel like kicking some demon ass?"

We shared a grin. "You know what?" he said, "I really, really do."

EPILOGUE

We stand on the hill overlooking the little cemetery behind the old mansion that's now my home. Not mother and daughter. Not today. Right now, we're just Kate and Allie, two Demon Hunters at the end of a battle.

We look down at the newest grave, the one where we'd interred Celia's ashes. Jared is down there again, sitting by the freshly turned earth, just as he has been every sunset for the last four days.

"He loved her." The words are quiet. Like a whisper. "He'd spent years looking for her. And he killed her to save me."

"She was already gone. He knew that."

"He couldn't be certain."

"Maybe. Maybe not. But he chose you. Can you live with that?"

"I don't know. I don't even know what it means. Does he love me? Because I think I love him."

"I know, baby. And it's going to be hard. And not just because he's a vampire. It was hard enough with me and your dad. For that matter, it was hard enough with me and Stuart."

"You're telling me all relationships are hard. I figured that out a long time ago. I'm pretty sure that's what YA novels are for. Especially the ones where a girl falls for a vampire."

"My smart, sarcastic girl." We share a laugh, and for a moment the heaviness of this moment disappears. "But it's not just about Jared. It's not even really about relationships. It's about this life. Because if you stay on this path, there are going to be other losses. More tragedies. You're going to lose people you love. You may even lose part of yourself. Are you prepared for that?"

"I don't know." The importance of this moment washes over me, and I stand taller as I draw a breath, then turn to face my mom. "But I know I'm not going to back away. This is who I am. And maybe Father Donnelly started something horrible back when Daddy was a baby. But maybe he started something good. Because of him, I can help people. Maybe even save the world. I have to try. Honestly, I want to."

She wipes away a tear and nods. "I know. It scares the crap out of me, but I know."

"You have to choose a path, too, you know. Not about Hunting. You already chose that. About Daddy. And Stuart. You have to tell him. You kept too many secrets."

"I know. I will." She turns to me with a sad smile. "It's hard, though. I love them both."

"Yeah. That's why I think it'll be okay."

"Have I mentioned how proud I am of you? How much I love you?"

"I love you, too, Mom," I tell her, then slide into her outstretched arms and lean in so I get the full force or her hug.

My name is Alison Elizabeth Crowe, and I'm a Demon Hunter, like my parents before me. And even though it's scary as hell, I can't wait to see where I go from here.

THE DEMON YOU KNOW

A
DEMON-HUNTING
SOCCER MOM
SHORT STORY

USA TODAY BESTSELLING AUTHOR
JULIE KENNER

M&O

I hope you enjoy this short story that falls chronologically between books four and five (*Deja Demon* and *Demon Ex Machina*).

XXOO
Julie

KATE

My name is Kate Connor, and I'm a suburban mom with a husband, a teenager, and a toddler. I'm also a Demon Hunter. And no, I don't mean that metaphorically. I really do hunt demons from Hell, although I thankfully don't have to go to Hell to do that. Instead, the demons come to me, and more often than I'd like, actually.

Demons, you might know, walk among us all the time. The air is, literally, filled with demonic essence living in the ether, a little fact that, frankly, can creep you out if you think about it too long. What's even creepier is that a demon's essence can also inhabit the body of a human. Sometimes the demon possesses the human, in which case you have a whole spinning-head, Linda Blair thing going on. That's not my area; for that, you call a priest.

More often (because what demon wants to walk around looking like the thing in *The Exorcist*?), a demon will move into a body at the moment of death, just as the human's soul is leaving. You've heard of those situations where someone is thought to be dead—a fall, a drowning —but then the victim is "miraculously" brought back to life.

Most of the time, that's no miracle. It's a demon. And one who brings with it strength beyond which the human had in life, not to mention a body that's pretty dang hard to kill. You want to off a demon, you have to stab it in the eye. Not as easy as it sounds, trust me on that, but pretty much any jab that punctures the sclera and reaches the vitreous humour will do. I've used knives, ice picks, barrettes, and even Happy Meal toys.

Manage to inflict that injury, and the demonic essence is sucked right back out into the ether.

Of course, demons can't pop into any old body. The souls of the faithful fight, and the window of opportunity passes pretty quickly. So it's not as if the world is overrun with demons walking around in human shells. But there are enough to keep me busy, and my fellow demon hunters, too. I work for Forza Scura, a super-secret arm of the Vatican, although I have to confess I haven't kept the secret quite as hush-hush as I should. My husband knows. My fourteen-year-old daughter Allie knows. My best friend Laura knows.

And it's quite possible my toddler knows, too, but he isn't saying.

Not that I'm completely incapable of keeping a secret. I haven't told the postman or the guy who runs the 7-11 on the corner. And although I know my martial arts instructor is curious about why a thirty-something mother of two can best him on the mat, so far I haven't succumbed to a whim and told him. Why? Because I am, more or less, capable of controlling my whims. Because I don't fly off the handle and do stupid things simply because my friends (or husband, or kids) want me to.

Responsibility.

Now there's a buzzword. And 'prudence.' And 'common sense.'

All qualities that a demon hunter needs to possess. Especially prudence. And clear, level-headed thinking. The ability to act fast in a crisis and not jump into a situation without first doing at least a basic assessment. All those are tools in a Hunter's toolbox, and as much as certain fourteen-year-olds might wish it were so, that particular skill set isn't acquired overnight. Which is why my particular fourteen-year-old, despite making serious strides on the knife-throwing and ass-kicking side of the equation, isn't yet going on regular patrols with her designated trainer. Namely, me.

A fact that has definitely raised the Teenage Sulk and Whine Meter in our house to Def Con One. And which, in a lovely bit of circular logic, completely justifies my refusal. Because if she was being clear-headed and prudent, she'd know that I was right—and there would be no whining, no angst, no moping about. Of course, when I tried *that* bit of logic on her, I was immediately assaulted with her standard reply of *Mother*, in a tone meant to express all sorts of unpleasant things, none of which it's prudent to say outright to your mom.

So maybe she's learned a little prudence after all...

I hoped so. Because right then she was in a situation that required the utmost common sense and prudence. And, possibly, a few ass-kicking skills, too.

Right then, my daughter Allie was on a date, or what I considered a date, although Allie swore it was nothing more than a group of friends going to the movies.

The entire lot had piled into my minivan earlier, and I'd driven them to the mall, the plan being to meet some other friends for dinner and a movie before the girls headed off to a sleepover, where another mom would get to deal with a gaggle of hormonally charged girls. The boys, presumably, would go home frustrated.

I remembered the way Jeremy's fingers had grazed Allie's back as they'd walked toward the mall entrance, the way Allie had smiled up at him, her lips soft and shiny from liberal applications of lipgloss (probably to make up for the fact that I'd refused to allow any other make-up).

She could call it a friendly movie outing all she wanted to, but I knew it was a date. My childhood might have been atypical, what with growing up in the Forza dorms and spending my Friday nights chasing preternatural vermin through the catacombs of Rome, but I was still a girl, and I'd been around the block more than once.

There are a lot of things that make moms nervous. The first time you leave your baby with a sitter. The first day of kindergarten. And, of course, the first time your daughter battles a demon right in her own backyard.

All those pale in comparison to an unchaperoned date, even one that technically isn't a date.

I took a sip of coffee and sighed. For the first time in ages I had the house to myself. My daughter was on a date. My husband had taken our toddler to see his parents. But I couldn't even enjoy the solitude.

Instead, all I could think as I sat in my kitchen, trying hard not to think at all, was that I hoped those talks about prudence and responsibility had gotten through my daughter's thick skull.

ALLIE

"**This is stupid,**" I shouted, trying to be heard over the music that filled the room and the bass beat that shook the floor. I held tight to the punch that Jeremy had brought me before sliding back into the throng of Coronado High students that filled the huge mansion's foyer. "We're going to get into so much trouble!"

"It's just a party, Al," Mindy said, leaning close so she didn't have to yell as loud. "It's not like we're doing anything bad." She said "bad" in the kind of voice that suggested backseats and kissing and the kind of stuff I'd never done before. And, honestly, didn't want to do yet, even though I could talk a good game in the girls' locker room. It wasn't like I was a prude or anything, but I wasn't sure I wanted that kind of hormonal rush yet. Besides, I didn't have the best of luck with boys. The first time I went out with a guy, he turned out to be a demon. The second time he was only a minion, but from my perspective, that was just as bad. Maybe worse. So pardon me if in my almost fifteen years of wisdom, I'm now thinking that maybe I should have my knife-fighting skills honed before I get in the backseat with a boy.

Not that I can explain any of that to Mindy. She doesn't know my mom's secret. And she sure doesn't know that I'm training to be a demon hunter, too.

I took a sip of my punch and almost spit it out. Whatever it had been spiked with tasted nasty. Not that the taste was slowing Mindy down.

"My mom would ground me for a year if she knew I was here, and you know your mom would, too."

She lifted a shoulder. "So?"

I love Mindy, don't get me wrong, but she's been kind of a pain lately. Her parents are getting divorced, so Mom says I'm supposed to be patient with her. But I wasn't entirely sure that meant that I was supposed to let her drag me to forbidden parties.

"You're not going to have fun if you don't relax a little," Mindy said. "Honestly, Allie. It's not like we're picking up guys on the beach or hitchhiking on the Coast Highway. It's a party. And everybody we know is here."

I took another sip of my drink, felt my head do a spinning thing, and saw Jeremy smiling at me from across the room. I wasn't sure I agreed with Mindy's assessment, but I had to admit that at the moment the perks were pretty good. Party. Friends. A boy who liked me. And, yeah, I know I had the whole justification thing going about so not needing a boyfriend, and so not wanting to deal with the stress of kisses and bodies and all that hormonal stuff, but at the same time, it's not like I could just flip a switch and not be fourteen anymore. I was a hormonal mess. I knew it, because not only did my mom spend half her life saying so, but also because I got the only A on our health quiz this semester. Trust me. All fourteen year olds are hormonal messes.

Jeremy made a beeline for me, his smile just shy enough to make my stomach do flip-flops. "Did you miss me?" he said. Like Mindy, he had to lean in close, and his breath tickled my ear. I caught Mindy's eye as Carson drew her away toward the makeshift dance floor. She wasn't saying anything, but was making embarrassing "go for it" expressions—embarrassing enough to make me think that she'd hit the punch bowl once too often.

Right as I was thinking that I needed to cut my best friend off, she stumbled over her own feet, a sure sign she was trashed. Instinctively, I took a step forward, but stopped right away, because someone caught her—and he wasn't Carson. Instead, he was an absolutely dreamy guy who couldn't have been more than sixteen years old. The kind of guy you see in magazines advertising deodorant soap, the idea being that if you don't stink, you can land a guy like that.

"Marlin Wheatley," Jeremy said, leaning close.

I didn't turn around. How could I, since that would mean I had to stop staring?

"No way is he in his twenties," I whispered, remembering what I'd been told about our host. "He's got to still be in high school."

Jeremy moved slightly, and I imagined he was shrugging. "Dunno. Guess he's just one of those guys."

I guessed so. One of those gorgeous, model-perfect, Greek-God-on-a-mountaintop kind of guys with a fabulous mansion overlooking the ocean, who throws awesome parties with cutting-edge music and tables and tables topped with amazing food and mindblowing drinks. Yeah. One of those guys.

Now, that guy was holding Mindy tight while she regained her balance. But he wasn't looking at her. Instead, he was looking right at me. There was something so familiar about his eyes. If I wanted to, I really thought I could float away in them.

Except part of me didn't want to. Part of me thought that would be a very bad idea. There was something about him...something deep in his eyes...

"Allie!"

I started, the movement breaking eye contact. I'd been thinking something...worrying about something, and I glanced back at Mindy, but she was upright and holding hands with Carson and everything seemed hunky-dory.

I turned to Jeremy, confused.

"Hey," he said. "Are you okay?"

"I..."

"You got this look. All worried and...I don't know." His brow furrowed. "You don't want to leave, do you?"

That knocked me back to reality. "I thought about it," I admitted. "My mom wouldn't exactly approve."

As far as Mom knew, the plan had been a movie

followed by a sleepover at Parker's house. (Parker is a girl, so that's not as risqué as it sounds.) The boys, of course, were not invited to that part of the evening.

"Forget this crap," Carson had said once we were safe inside the mall. "Tonight's Marlin Wheatley's party."

"Who?" I'd asked, and they'd all looked at me like I was from Mars. Turns out, Wheatley's some rich twenty-something computer bazillionaire who'd moved to the area a few months ago and has been talking up this party for ages.

"Why?"

Jeremy and Parker had looked at each other and shrugged. "Don't know. Guess he wants to make sure people come."

"But why throw it in the first place?"

"He's a college drop-out geek. This is probably his way of meeting girls. Who cares, anyway? It's a party."

I probably could have said something, but I didn't, and after about thirty minutes, we pulled up in front of the biggest house I'd ever seen. I had no idea where we were, other than that we were on one of the cliffs over-looking the Pacific in a mega-ritzy neighborhood I'd never seen before. Walking to the front door, I could smell the ocean, and the lights of the house seemed magical against the black night sky.

At that one moment, I had absolutely no hesitation about blowing off the movie and sneaking off to a party.

Inside, when I'd smelled the alcohol in the punch and saw the guy I share a lab table with in biology barf into a potted plant, the second thoughts set in.

Still, there was nothing inherently bad about a barfing lab partner, right? Just because he drank too much didn't mean I would. And I couldn't deny the biggest, most glaring fact of all—I really liked the way Jeremy was looking at me. If I was a widdle girl who made a phone call to her mommy, would he ever look at me that way again?

"Earth to Allie," he said. "Come on. Don't do that to me. Tell me you don't want to leave."

"No," I said, not realizing until that moment that I was certain. "I don't want to leave."

He pressed his hands over his heart and pretended to swoon. "Saved," he said. "I was expecting a mortal blow."

I laughed, and thought that felt pretty darn nice.

Mom might not think I was ready to make decisions in the field, but we weren't talking demons here. This was a party. And just because she was a demon hunter didn't mean she could go in and hijack all of my decisions from me. I was fourteen years old! I was supposed to be going to parties with friends. I'm pretty sure that's in the rule book somewhere.

"I'm staying," I said again, just because I liked the way it sounded. Then I smiled up at Jeremy. "In fact, I think I want more punch."

"You're Allie, right?"

I dropped the dipper back into the bowl, splattering

the pink liquid onto my shirt, as I looked up to find
Marlin smiling at me from the kitchen doorway.

"Sorry," he said silkily. "I didn't mean to startle you."

"No, you..." I trailed off because, hey, he had startled
me. What was the point of denying it?

He nodded toward the bowl. "You like the punch."

"Yes," I lied. Actually, I'd come into the kitchen
hoping to find something in the refrigerator to drink
instead. I'd lucked out, too. The punch was apparently a
mixture of pink lemonade, Sprite, and some unidentifi-
able alcohol of the wow-is-that-strong variety. I didn't
like it. And so I'd filled my cup to the brim with plain old
pink lemonade, and then had gone to the punch bowl to
do a color comparison.

Yes, I know I should simply be able to say, "No, I
don't like the punch," or, "Gee, the alcohol in the punch
is making my head swim." Instead, I was going to silently
lie by carrying around a big cup of my own version of
punch. Cowardly, maybe, but it would keep me sober. I
might be defying Mom by staying at the party, but
getting drunk on top of that? If she found out, I'd be
grounded until my wedding night. Which I wouldn't
have, because she'd never let me near a guy again.

A slow grin spread across Marlin's face, and those
odd eyes twinkled as he peered at the clear plastic tumbler
filled with pink lemonade that I now held—a tumbler
that was about the size of four of the cups that were piled
high in the foyer next to the punch bowl. "I think I have
a bigger glass if you'd like."

I lifted my chin and hoped I looked like a high school

student defending her right to drink spiked punch. "No thanks. I've already had a lot. This is just about perfect."

He moved closer, although his voice seemed to stay very far away. His hand touched my back, and I had the oddest sensation that his fingers were going right through me. I tried to stifle a shiver but didn't quite manage.

"Problem?" he asked, his voice slick and oily, his breath so minty I had to assume he wasn't drinking the punch.

"Cold punch," I said. "Brain freeze."

"Ah." He put pressure on my back, and like a dutiful puppy, I moved forward. "I was looking for you. Mindy and Carson and Jeremy joined me in the study along with a few more of your friends. Will you join us? It's less boisterous than the foyer and ballroom, but easier to talk."

"Sure," I said. In some part of my mind, I recognized that he spoke strangely, his words overly formal or something. But I couldn't really think about it. I tried a bit, but the thoughts wouldn't stick, and by the time we reached the study, I'd forgotten all about it.

The room was oak-paneled and fancy, like something out of an old movie, and I looked around, taking in the paintings in gilt frames, the ornate furniture on which my friends and a bunch of other kids were sitting, and the massive wooden desk.

I saw Carson and Jeremy on a sofa, just sitting and talking. Mindy was on an overstuffed loveseat nursing another cup of punch. She looked up at me, her eyes glassy and her smile crooked, and I started toward her, determined to cut her off.

I'd taken one step when it happened—the room changed. The formal-looking study disappeared in a snap and suddenly I was in a room filled with nothing but red and black. Blood, I realized, and it coated the walls, the scent of it filling my nose and making me want to gag.

Something squished under my feet, and I looked down to find myself tromping on maggots, their fat little bodies bursting beneath my shoes.

And right in front of me, the big wooden desk was now a giant stone slab, like the kind ancient tribes used to make sacrifices to the gods.

Oh God, oh God, oh God...

I closed my eyes and tried to breathe normally, and when I opened them again—slowly and tentatively—the room was completely back in order.

What the heck?

I glanced at the lemonade in my hand. Maybe I should have cut myself off sooner.

On the couch, Mindy was peering at me, her forehead crinkled. I must have looked freaked, because she pushed herself up and started toward me. She, at least looked normal. At least that's what I thought at first. Then I saw the weird tentacle things that were wrapped around her ankles and wrists. She, however, didn't seem aware of them at all. And I sure as heck didn't understand why I was seeing them.

I blinked again, and the tentacles disappeared, but the blood was back. Then the tentacles were, and I stood there hyperventilating as I realized that the long, gray squid-like arms were attached to all the kids, and that they extended back to Marlin, who'd taken a seat behind the blood-soaked sacrificial stone. I mean the desk. The slab. The desk.

I had no idea why I was seeing two versions of the same room, one very decidedly coming at me straight from the Horror Channel. But I did know with absolute certainty that Marlin was a demon. I mean, that was the only explanation, right? And his minty-fresh breath was a big, minty clue. Too minty. I should have realized; hadn't mom trained me to notice breath? And didn't demons have the nastiest breath imaginable? The kind of breath that they would mask with liberal doses of mouthwash and tons and tons of minty candies.

Oh, shit.

The room was changing with every glance, as if I was looking at one of those holographic bubblegum cards that change slightly depending on the angle.

"Allie?" Mindy asked. "Are you okay?"

"I...no. My head feels weird." What was I supposed to say? Did you know there's a squid creature attached to you, and it's Marlin? "I think it must be the drink."

I think it must be the drink...

That was it! I was absolutely, positively certain of it. Everyone in that room except me was drunk on punch, and none of the kids in that room saw what I was seeing —and what I was seeing was reality mixed in with a little bit of a mirage. Only it was the blood that was the reality, along with the tentacles and the maggots. And the stone table.

The oak paneled study was the fantasy—and the punch induced it. It was spiked with more than alcohol, that was for sure.

But I'd stopped drinking the punch, so I wasn't drunk, even though Marlin had invited me in because he assumed I was. I only had a little bit of demon juice in me, and so I could see what the room really looked like... and I was scared to death.

Once more, I'd gone on a date, and been sucked into demon-ville. I mean, that's all great and fabulous once I'm a demon hunter, but right now, I'm a high school student, and it's not like I've got my knife in my itty bitty purse.

In fact, all I had in my purse that could even remotely pass for a weapon was nail clippers.

I drew in a breath for courage, and decided that one tiny pair of clippers would just have to do.

Then I saw two more tentacles sliding across the floor heading straight toward me, and I knew that nail clippers weren't the answer. I wasn't ready for this. How could I fight this?

Mom.

The tentacles were only a few feet away now, and I clapped my hand over my mouth, mumbled something about needing to throw up, and turned and raced out the door.

I didn't know where I was or what I was going to do, but I knew I had to find someplace safe, then hole up and call my mom, so I pulled open the first door I found and lunged into a dingy, dust-covered bedroom filled with moldy, decaying furniture and a stench that made me want to really throw up.

I ignored it and pulled out my cell phone and my nail clippers. I jabbed my finger on the speed dial number for home, then opened the clippers and extended the metal file, giving me a weapon that extended about one and a half inches. In other words, completely freaking useless for self-defense against most creatures, but deadly to a demon if I could put that point through his eye. The trick, of course, was not getting dead first.

On the other end of the line, the phone rang.

"Come on, come on..."

One ring, then another and another until finally, "Hello?"

"Mom!"

That was all I said. Because right then Marlin burst through the door, yanked the phone out of my hand, and hurled it through the window. Glass shattered under the force, but I barely heard the noise. Instead, all I was hearing was my own screams.

"So you know," Marlin said, his mouth moving, but a deeper voice coming out. "It matters not. This year's sacrifices have been chosen. Your failure to drink fully of the elixir is of no consequence. What you have seen does not matter. The dead tell no tales, Alison, and you cannot stop us. Judemore will rise. He will feed. And he will bestow his bounty upon me for yet another year."

He said all of that, and then he smiled. And before I

even had time to think that I really didn't like the look of that smile, he lunged.

And guess what? I was right. My nail clippers with their tiny metal file were no match against Marlin. I needed a knife. A gun. A Civil War replica sword. Something—anything—to fight with.

I had nada though, so I hauled out every martial arts trick I'd learned, and I few that I made up right there on the fly—but he was one hell of a lot tougher than me, and I wasn't even slowing him down.

I wanted to cry with frustration. More, I wanted to cry with anger—at myself for being such a complete and total idiot. For coming here. For doing everything wrong. And for getting myself, my best friend, and a bunch of kids killed.

Because that was what was going to happen. I knew it the moment Marlin hauled me off the floor and carried me kicking and screaming and beating and fighting into the study. I knew when he tied me to a blood-soaked chair.

I knew when he didn't pry my fingers open and take my tiny nail clippers, leaving them instead as a symbol of what I couldn't accomplish no matter how hard I tried.

Tears streamed down my cheeks, and I tried to listen to what Marlin was saying, but I couldn't hear through the rush of my fear.

Right then, I wanted my mom, and not in a way most kids want a parent when they were in trouble.

I wanted my mom to burst through those doors and kick some demon ass.

But I knew she wouldn't. I'd barely said a word. She probably didn't even realize I was in trouble.

I'd messed up. Big time.

And I wasn't even going to be around to get grounded for it.

Something hard and tight locked around my heart and my breath felt fluttery and hot. Fear.

I didn't want to die.

But right then, I really didn't think that I had a choice.

KATE

Not good, I thought, as I desperately tried to call Allie back. Frantic calls from your daughter that end abruptly are never a good thing.

No answer. For that matter, no ring. The phone went straight to voice mail.

My stomach twisted with worry. I should never have let her go to the mall. What was I thinking? Malls were dangerous. Hell, the world was dangerous. Who knew that better than me?

As my mind churned, my fingers were busy looking up Parker's phone number, then dialing, then tapping out a rhythm on the counter as I waited for a ring, then an answer.

Finally, a sleepy voice came on the line.

"Is Allie okay?" I asked without preamble.

A pause, during which every dark fear I'd ever known bubbled up inside me.

"Who?"

"Allie!" I shouted. "My daughter. She's there with Parker and Mindy."

"Kate?" I heard the confusion in Rhonda Downing's voice. "What are you talking about? Parker and the girls are sleeping over at Tanya's house." In the silence that followed, I heard her understanding. "Aren't they?"

"Call," I said sharply. "Call and find out."

I slammed the phone down, because I already knew what the answer was. The girls weren't at Tanya's anymore than they were at Parker's. They'd planned and plotted to go somewhere, though, and now they were in trouble, and I didn't have any way to find them.

Think, dammit, think.

I didn't even know if the trouble was of the human or the demon variety. Not that it mattered. I was going to find them, I was going to save them, and then I was going to ground my daughter until college.

First, I had to find her.

How? They could be anywhere. All I knew was that she had her phone, or at least was near it. Maybe I could triangulate the phone signal? They did that in the movies, right? So maybe if I called Rome, someone at Forza could—

Mindy.

I didn't need Forza—for that matter I wasn't even sure if my Hollywood triangulation plan would work. But I knew that I could track Mindy.

But were they together? Dear God, please let them be together.

I raced toward the back door, then sprinted across the back yard to Laura's house. My best friend is also Mindy's mom, and they live in the house directly behind us, which makes it convenient for moments like these. Not that my heart could stand many moments like these.

"Does Mindy have her iPhone?" I asked after pushing my way inside, past Laura who stood blinking and sleepy in a bathrobe. The phone had been a guilt-loaded present designed to lessen the emotional trauma of the divorce. Mindy had been thrilled, and Laura had justified the purchase by pointing out the cool feature that let you go onto the Internet to find a lost phone—or, presumably, track down the missing child who was holding it. "I need to know where she is!"

Horror crossed her face and I realized belatedly that I could have approached the whole "our daughters are in danger" thing a little more gently. To Laura's credit, however, she didn't interrogate me until she was already at the computer.

I barely had time to tell her what happened when a map appeared on screen showing the location of the phone. "I'm off," I said. I'd grabbed my favorite jacket on my way out the door, so I had my stiletto in the sleeve and another knife in my purse, along with a bottle of holy water. I also keep supplies under the front seat of my minivan, but I didn't want to waste time going back to my house.

"Take my car," Laura said, when I'd told her as much. "And bring my baby back." She sounded brave, but I could see the worry on her face and knew it reflected my own.

"I will," I said, and I meant it. I only hoped I could do it. More than that, I hoped that Allie was still with Mindy.

That, however, wasn't something I could worry about. This was the only lead I had. Allie had to be there, and I raced west toward the cliffs that overlooked the coast, maneuvering my way up into one of San Diablo's ritzier neighborhoods until I finally found the address where Mindy's phone now was.

Immediately, I knew I had the right place. There were cars everywhere, and teenagers littering the lawn and massive front porch. The fear that had gripped me loosened a little. Maybe this wasn't life-or-death after all. Maybe she'd gone to a frat party. Maybe she'd dropped the phone.

Maybe I needed to get inside that house and find out for myself.

Inside, I found more kids, more eating, more music, more drinking.

But I didn't find Allie or Mindy.

I glanced around, frantic, not sure where to even start looking. The place was huge.

As if in answer, a scream ripped through the room, cutting through even the din of the party. I couldn't have been the only one who heard it, and yet I was the only one who reacted, and I was sprinting up the stairs, heading for the source, before the echo of the sound had died out.

What I found turned me cold.

A baby-faced man standing in the center of an oak-paneled study, arms outstretched, his body bathed in red, his skin bulging and popping as something within him rose and grew. And, yeah, I knew what that something was: a demon.

He was surrounded by about a dozen kids sitting casually around the room, not freaking out or even reacting despite the writhing, changing thing in the middle. All the kids, including Mindy, who had a goofy smile on her face. Everyone, that is, except Allie—she was tied to a chair, and my heart twisted when I saw her. I, however, forced myself to concentrate on my goal: killing the demon.

This was not your run-of-the-mill body-inhabiting demon, and yet I'd heard of this kind of thing. Young men who gave themselves body and soul to a demon in order to gain power and never-ending youth. To keep it up, though, they had to make constant sacrifices.

The human/demon hadn't even noticed me as far as I could tell. The rising had thrust it into a trance, but I guessed that wouldn't last long. Soon the awakening would be complete, and it would want to feed. And that, I thought, was where all the kids came in.

I needed to take advantage of the trance. I needed to kill the thing right then, and I raced forward to do just that.

"Mom!" Allie screamed. "Be careful! You can't see it, but he's a demon, and he's—"

"I can see him," I said, tackling the beast and knocking him to the floor. This was going to be too easy.

"Really?" She was so incredulous she almost sounded normal. "What about the room? The tentacles?"

"Tentacles?" I'd been poised to jab my stiletto through his eye. Now I hesitated.

"He's holding onto the kids. All of us. Me, too," she said, glancing down at her ankles as if in support of her statement. "There was punch, but I only drank a little, and I could see what was real and they couldn't and—"

"I get it," I said, though I didn't completely. I got enough. The kids who'd drunk the punch must see the demon as I saw him, they just weren't afraid. Because they were part of it now. Part of the ceremony, part of the world. Kill the demon, and they'd step up to fight. Either that, or they'd die, too.

To ensure the kids stayed alive (and to make sure they didn't become demonic fighting minions), we had to cut the tentacles before we killed the beast. And since I couldn't see them...

I jumped off the demon and raced toward Allie, who was screaming questions at me. I sliced the ropes that bound her, then handed her the larger knife. "Cut them," I said. "Cut all the tentacles. I can't kill him until the kids are free."

Her eyes went wide, but she didn't hesitate. Didn't question, and despite the fact that I was beyond furious with her for sneaking off to a party, right then, I was pretty damn proud.

Quickly, she reached down and sliced through the

tentacles that bound her. When she did, the demon I'd left on the floor shook with life.

Damn. I'd been afraid of that.

"I'll keep you safe," I said, racing back to the demon. "Hurry!"

She'd sliced through another tentacle by the time I got back to the demon. I landed a solid punch to its bulbous, writhing face. I risked a sideways look and saw a boy who'd been sitting calmly in a chair sink to the floor in a dead faint. Good. I'd rather a roomful of kids not see this.

Another set of tentacles cut, and this time the force of the break brought the demon to life. He leaped up, knocking me off him before turning to attack Allie. I tackled him, buying her time to slice through another, as the demon twisted and kicked, and I blocked and parried.

I had my stiletto and damned if I didn't want to use it. Fighting was easier when you were going for the kill. Trying to slow things down was hard. And painful, I thought, when he picked me up and hurled me toward the desk. I landed hard on my back, my breath going out of me, but I didn't have time to think about the pain. Allie had reached the last kid—the last set of tentacles.

Mindy.

But the demon was on his way there, too.

No way.

I lunged, knocking him down before he could get to Mindy. I screamed for Allie to hurry, fighting to position myself as she hacked at the last two tentacles.

"Now!" she yelled, and I lashed down with my stiletto—and as I did, the demon thrust out his arm, knocking the blade from my hand and sending it skittering across the room. Shit!

I clutched his wrist, my knees clamped tight as I straddled him, but I couldn't hold him for long. I needed a weapon, something I could slide into his eye—something sharp and pointy that could kill a demon.

"Mom!" Allie said, and as she spoke, she tossed me something small and silver. Instinctively, the demon tilted his head up and opened his eyes wide.

And that was all it took.

I snatched the clippers from the air, held them with the pointy file sticking out, and plunged the metal deep into the demon's eye.

Immediately, I heard the hiss of the demon leaving the body. Beneath me, all that was left was a shell.

A dead body.

And there I was in a roomful of kids, all of whom would surely awake from their faints soon enough.

I sighed. A dead body wasn't going to go over well with them.

Lamenting the fact that demons don't disappear in a puff of ash and smoke, I grabbed the body under the arms and started dragging it. "Open it," I said to Allie, motioning with my head to a door at the back of the room.

She ran ahead, and I shoved the body into the small, dark closet. For now, that would have to be enough, especially since there was no time to do more.

Around us, all the kids were stirring. I saw Jeremy's eyes go wide, then saw him look around frantically, relaxing when his eyes found Allie.

"What happened?" he mumbled.

"You should go home, Jeremy," I said, then looked around at the entire group. "All of you."

Faced with a disapproving adult, they all slunk out guiltily. All except Mindy, who was looking at me with no small amount of trepidation. "Hi, Aunt Kate," she said. She cleared her throat, then turned her attention to Allie. "We're in a lot of trouble, aren't we?"

Allie cocked her head to the side and looked at me, her eyebrows raised in question, as if the fact that she'd done herself proud in the demonic ass-kicking department would erase all the other wrongs of the night.

I didn't answer. After a minute, that was answer enough.

Allie sighed. But not her usual exasperated sigh. This one was a sigh of resignation and acceptance, and I knew then that although the lesson had been hard fought, she'd learned a bit more about prudence and responsibility tonight.

"We're definitely in trouble," her words said, and I know that's what Mindy heard. But what I heard was, "I love you, Mom."

"I love you, too, kid," I whispered. "Now let's go home."

ABOUT THE AUTHOR

Julie Kenner (aka J. Kenner) is the *New York Times*, *USA Today*, *Publishers Weekly*, *Wall Street Journal* and #1 International bestselling author of over one hundred novels, novellas and short stories in a variety of genres.

Stay in touch with JK and be the first to know about new releases: **Just text: JKenner to 21000 to subscribe to JK's text alerts or follow her on social using @juliekenner**